T3-BOP-680

"Where do you think she is?"
the cartel thug asked with diffidence.

"I don't know. She can't be far—somewhere in the arroyo."

Jessie, lying with her cheek pressed to the earth not twenty feet from the searchers, could see the fire continuing to roar along the edge of the plateau. She shuddered at the thought of them setting fire to the arroyo where she hid.

"Oh, Ki, where are you?"

Perhaps he couldn't save her; perhaps he was already dead, but all of this would be easier to face with Ki, with imperturbable, sturdy Ki. But Ki wasn't there and he didn't hear her whispered words or the choked groan in her throat as the cartel men approached the arroyo with lighted torches...

◆━ WESLEY ELLIS ━◆

LONE STAR

AND THE APACHE WARRIOR

A JOVE BOOK

LONE STAR AND THE APACHE WARRIOR

A Jove Book/published by arrangement with
the author

PRINTING HISTORY
Jove edition/September 1985

All rights reserved.
Copyright © 1985 by Jove Publications, Inc.
This book may not be reproduced in whole or in part,
by mimeograph or any other means, without permission.
For information address: The Berkley Publishing Group,
200 Madison Avenue, New York, N.Y. 10016.

ISBN: 0-515-08344-5

Jove books are published by The Berkley Publishing Group,
200 Madison Avenue, New York, N.Y. 10016. The words
"A JOVE BOOK" and the "J" with sunburst are trademarks
belonging to Jove Publications, Inc.

PRINTED IN THE UNITED STATES OF AMERICA

LONE STAR

AND THE
APACHE WARRIOR

Chapter 1

The train carried them as far as Tucson. From there they traveled by coach across the raw, red desert to Fort Bowie, Arizona Territory.

They were an unusual pair, this young honey-blond woman with a figure that would make a sculptor weep and the tall, dark, Oriental man she traveled with. The other passengers eyed them speculatively. The woman in her green riding jacket and skirt, flat brown Stetson and silk blouse drew most of the attention from the men. With good reason. Green-eyed, molded to perfection, she would have been a standout anywhere. Here in this godforsaken country, which was nothing but a nest for rattlers, scorpions, and Apache Indians, she was a rarity almost beyond belief. Now and then the tall Oriental spoke to her. He called her Jessica.

The Oriental, too, was a mystery. At first the drummer riding the stage had thought him to be an Indian, but a closer inspection changed his mind. The tall man was wearing a blue-gray suit, blue shirt, and string tie. He had a light colored Stetson fitted on his head and a pair of polished but dusty Wellingtons on his feet. He spoke without a noticeable accent. When the woman spoke to him, she called him Ki.

"Goin' all the way to Bowie?" the drummer, whose name was Farnsworth, asked, leaning forward to be a little nearer to the woman.

"All the way, yes," Jessica Starbuck answered.

"It's not much of a place," Farnsworth said somewhat morosely. He himself was in deep trouble with the home office and for punishment had been given the Arizona and New Mexico Territories as his parish. "I'm in ladies's apparel," he added, which drew a searching look from the fourth passenger, a hard-faced cavalry captain with an unkempt, reddish mustache.

"You got people in the army, Miss?" the officer asked now. "Pardon me—everyone else seems to be introducing himself—the name's Bourke, Jeff Bourke."

"Happy to meet you. No, I have no one in the army," Jessica answered. The wind had drifted a strand of pale hair across her face and now she swept it back.

"It's just that not many people voluntarily go to Bowie," the captain went on. The drummer gave him a concurring glance. "Well..." Bourke's voice trailed off. "Just trying to make conversation."

Jessica smiled and nodded, but she didn't answer. She looked out the window at the red desert, the distant hills, Apache Pass, where Fort Bowie was situated. No, not many would voluntarily travel to Fort Bowie in these times. Not with Firesky wandering around raiding, looting, murdering. They had heard about the Chiricahua Apache war leader back in Tucson. He was as clever as Cochise, they said, and as resilient as Geronimo.

The trouble had started with the Apaches.

2

There was a large Indian reservation near Fort Bowie and it was primarily populated by Apaches—those who had surrendered, been taken prisoner, or given up. The trouble was they were threatening now to break out.

"There," Captain Bourke said, pointing out the window. "You can take a look, Miss. That's Firesky's work. You can bet on it."

Jessica leaned forward, hanging on to the strap beside the stagecoach door. Distantly she could see a column of black smoke rising into the clear Arizona sky.

"Apaches?" Ki asked.

"Who else? Yes, Firesky most likely."

"What's over there?" Jessie wanted to know. There was no wind out on the desert. The smoke rose like an accusing finger pointing directly at the pale sky.

"Gordon Stamper has a place there. Small rancher. Looks like maybe I should say he *had* a place there," Bourke amended grimly. He leaned back and after another minute so did Jessie.

"How are things on the reservation?" Jessica asked the army captain.

His red eyebrows drew together. "How do you come to know about that? Who are you anyway? Not Bureau of Indian Affairs by any chance?"

"No," Jessie assured him, "not that." The captain relaxed a little. It seemed he was wary of civilians coming on the post, on the reservation.

He shrugged. "There's been some trouble," Bourke admitted. "A few young bucks have broken out and joined up with Firesky."

"Why is that?" Ki asked, although he knew the answer. The captain shrugged again.

"They want to fight. They're bored with reservation life. You know Indians."

3

Ki nodded ambiguously and looked at Jessica who had taken her hat off and shaken her shiny hair free. She was deep in thought now, looking worried but eager—knowing she was nearing the source of a problem that was plaguing the reservations across the southwest. Or so she hoped.

She was, Ki thought, remarkably beautiful on this day. She was always so when there was a chance they would do battle. Her eyes lighted softly with an animal intensity, which was exquisitely feminine yet dangerous in its implications.

She was dangerous. Dangerous and beautiful at once. Ki knew that she only appeared vulnerable. Beneath her tweed skirt was a holster strapped to her smooth white thigh and in the holster a twin barrel .38 caliber derringer with ivory grips. It wasn't there for decoration. Jessica Starbuck knew when and how to use it. She also knew enough in the way of *te*—barehanded fighting learned from Ki—to back down most men.

It was necessity that had forced this sort of knowledge to become a part of the woman sitting next to Ki, the woman who smelled faintly of lilac powder. She had become a warrior because there was no one else to do battle.

Her father had been a great man, a powerful man, but like many powerful men he had had enemies. The cartel which had murdered Alex Starbuck had worldwide resources and absolutely no scruples. They couldn't have expected this soft, young woman to prove herself such a thorn in the side, but then they didn't know what a determined lady she was. With the cartel responsible for her parents' deaths she had taken a vow, a vow to use all the resources of the Starbuck empire to strike down the many-headed snake that was the cartel. She had many weapons, economic as well as physical, but none so valuable as her personal courage—none so important as Ki. Ki who was ready to

4

lay down his life for her. Ki who was of *te,* who was a warrior without peer. Ki who knew the soft ways of killing.

"Another fire," Captain Bourke said. "Nearer the post, it seems. If those bastards..."

Ki never heard the report of the first shot, but he saw its effect. The bullet whipped through the flimsy wall of the coach, splintering it wildly, the wall not even slowing the bullet. It passed on through Bourke's neck while the cavalry officer was leaning forward, looking out the window.

Blood spewed from Bourke's mouth. He lifted a finger, pointed out the window, then slumped to the floor, dead.

"Get down," Ki shouted, grabbing the drummer by the collar, yanking him toward him and onto the floor where he lay pressed against the dead officer. They could hear the shots now and the war whoops. From a bag at her feet Jessica Starbuck pulled a Colt revolver, a .38 caliber weapon mounted on a heavier .44 frame.

The Indian who came abreast of the stagecoach whooping and waving his rifle was blown from his pony's back. Smoke curled from the muzzle of the Colt.

From an inside pocket Ki took three small, deadly throwing stars—*shuriken.* They heard and felt the impact of a body landing on the roof and saw an Indian lean down, peer in, and poke his pistol into the coach. Ki leaped for the Apache's wrist, yanked and twisted. The Apache fell from the roof and screamed as the rear wheel ran over him.

The coach bounced high in the air, went up on two wheels and then tilted, tumbling wildly in a tangle of horse, harness, human bodies, and dust.

Before the coach had settled on its side Ki was out of the door. The Apache to his right had his rifle sighted on Ki, but the *shuriken* in Ki's hand moved first. The Indian could never have seen it coming or imagined it to be a death-dealing thing.

5

With seeming careless ease Ki flipped the razor-edged star toward the Chiricahua, turning his attention away before the *shuriken* had imbedded itself in the Indian's throat, tearing trachea and jugular open, causing the warrior to strangle on his own blood.

Ki heard Jessie's Colt fire again and from the corner of his eye saw a pony tumble, throwing its rider. There were three attackers left. The first fell to a *shuriken,* the second veered off, avoiding a shot from Jessica's pistol.

The third charged directly at them. He was stocky, scarred, weirdly painted with mescal juice and deer blood, his face blacked out with soot. The Apache had a war lance in his hands and fire in his eyes. He leaped from his pony to the overturned stage.

He landed softly, like a big cat and his first strike, an upthrusting blow with his war lance should have been a good one. But the Apache had never met a master of *te* before and the elation on his face faded to dismayed shock as Ki sidestepped gracefully, gripped the lance behind the head, and pulled. The Apache was jerked off balance and he had to let go of the weapon.

That didn't mean he was ready to give it up. From his waistband he drew a long, narrow knife. Sunlight glinted on the blade as the Indian crouched, glancing once at Jessie who was frantically reloading and then back to Ki who was standing turned slightly, hands loosely poised before him. The stance reminded the Apache of something but he didn't remember for a moment. Then he knew—it was an eagle, talons ready to strike, wings spread. The Chiricahua shook the image off.

"No," Ki said softly. "Do not do this. The fight is over. Do not die."

The Indian hissed something and dived at Ki, trying to

6

plunge the knife into the tall man's heart. The blade never got there.

The Apache felt light pressure on his wrist and behind his elbow and then he was flying through the air, landing roughly against the sandy earth, his own knife in his belly. He tried to rise and could not. He turned his head and saw the man standing above him, then he saw the eagle winging away into a fiery sky. The Apache saw nothing else but the Void.

"Dead?" The drummer was peering up out of the coach.

Ki looked at him with dark, unreadable eyes. "Yes, he is dead."

"They all gone?" The drummer pulled himself up onto the side of the coach, puffing a little with the effort. He had lost his derby and Ki noticed that the man was almost entirely bald. He stood on the coach next to Ki and scanned the desert. "Gone."

They were gone, but it made no sense to Ki, not until he saw the dust moving toward them minutes later—the riders of the horses wore blue and carried the colors of the U.S. cavalry.

The drummer, Farnsworth, began waving his arms like windmills. Ki went to Jessica Starbuck who was standing, pistol dangling from her right hand, the wind twisting her honey-blond hair, pressing her silk blouse to her breasts revealingly.

"You are all right?"

"Yes, Ki. That was quite an introduction to Arizona."

"We are fortunate, I think," Ki said. "If the cavalry hadn't been nearby, it could have been bad."

"Let's be grateful that it wasn't." She looked into the distances. "There's too much to do."

"Yes. Far too much." Ki looked at Jessie until she became

7

aware of his gaze and looked at him directly with those frank green eyes. Then the tall man said, "I'll retrieve our possessions. All the luggage is scattered across the land."

"The driver?" Jessie asked, already knowing the answer.

"Dead."

Then Ki leaped nimbly down and began trudging back along their trail, searching for their lost baggage. He inconspicuously removed the *shuriken* from the body of the Apache warrior. It did no good for people to see curious things. The word of their arrival would all too soon reach the cartel.

Jessie had climbed down from the coach without the help of Farnsworth who had viewed the occasion as an opportunity to get his hands on her deliciously contoured rear end. A scathing glance had dissuaded the drummer.

The cavalry contingent had lifted its horses into a gallop at the sight of the overturned stagecoach and now they were quickly closing the gap. By the time Jessica had retrieved her hat, swept back her hair, and put her pistol away the yellow-legs had arrived.

Their officer was a young blond lieutenant with strikingly clear blue eyes, tanned cheeks, square shoulders, and slightly long sideburns. He drew up in a cloud of dust, his hand held high to halt the patrol behind him.

He swung down and before the dust had settled he was beside Jessica Starbuck.

"Miss, are you all right?" He had a pleasant baritone voice and the inflections of New England. His eyes met Jessica's and his expression changed from one of concern to one of interest. Jessie saw the sparks dance in the young officer's eyes, saw him stiffen and straighten.

"Everything's all right now. You might help *him* down," she said, nodding toward Farnsworth.

"All right." The lieutenant was looking around. He saw

8

the driver now lying beneath the coach, crushed and quite dead. "There was supposed to be an officer on the coach."

"Captain Bourke. He's dead," Jessie said.

The captain gave a few rapid orders to his men and two of them swung down to clamber into the coach to retrieve the dead captain's body. Ki had returned by then, carrying Jessie's trunk on his shoulders and his own worn leather satchel in his left hand. The lieutenant's eyes narrowed slightly.

"And who might you be?" he asked.

Ki didn't like the question much. He couldn't see that it was any business of the lieutenant's who he was. Nevertheless he answered.

"They call me Ki."

"You're with this woman?"

"That's right."

It was the lieutenant's turn to be nettled. He didn't much care to discover that this white woman was traveling with a Chinaman.

"They're putting distance between us, sir," a stocky sergeant said, nodding toward the south in the direction the Apaches had gone.

"We'll not catch them today, Masters." Lieutenant White removed his hat and wiped his forehead with a folded handkerchief.

"You'll have to ride in with us," he told Jessie. He was smiling as he spoke. His eyes were still roving her body, caressing her. "We've extra mounts."

"Fine," Jessie said. She flashed another smile and the lieutenant was her slave. "If you're ready then . . . ?"

In minutes they were mounted, their baggage and the dead loaded on pack animals, Farnsworth sitting astride a mule captured or collected somewhere.

They turned southward, Ki and Jessie riding near the

front, keeping a few lengths between themselves and the cavalry officer.

Ki was frowning as he watched White's back. Jessie reached across and poked his shoulder. "What's the matter, don't you like him?"

"I don't dislike him," Ki said tactfully.

"I don't either. Dislike him. He pulled us out of a pretty bad spot anyway."

"Do you intend to go into the fort with them?" Ki wanted to know.

"No. Not now. I want to find Corson and get things straightened out."

"Yes. The Sunset Ranch was it?"

"That's what he called it. People will know where it is."

"You know, Jessica, there isn't much time." Ki was still looking at the distant smoke. "If we don't solve this, there'll be more killing. Much more. The territory will be soaked in blood."

"Then," Jessie answered. "We'd better solve it. And fast."

Chapter 2

Jessie and Ki rented two horses in the crumbling, tilted town of Bowie, which stood in the shadow of the fort. Lieutenant White had tried valiantly to dissuade Jessica.

"You can't be serious, Miss Starbuck. You need rest—after the day you've had today."

"I need to see Champ Corson, Lieutenant. We have urgent business."

"What sort of business could possibly be this urgent?" White asked. If they had answered him directly, he probably wouldn't have believed them anyway, and so Jessica didn't.

"It *is* urgent, that's all there is to it."

"With the Apaches roaming around out there..."

"Do you know where the Sunset Ranch is?" Jessica asked, interrupting.

"Yes." White sighed. "Six miles out. South of town. They call the area Horn Canyon. You can't miss it if you take the road and stay on it."

"Thank you," Jessie had told him and she had turned away. White, however, wasn't ready to give it up.

"Will I see you again—later—when you've finished with your business?" he had asked hopefully.

Jessie gave that hope a little support. "I hope so," she smiled. "Yes, I do hope so, Lieutenant."

Now the sky had begun to go purple and russet as Ki and Jessica approached the ranch which sat in the middle of a broad, dry grass valley. There was no water to be seen anywhere, as there was none anywhere in the country, but the cattle and horses they passed seemed fat and sleek. There were, however, very few cattle, not more than two dozen on all the broad range.

"Those are just his breeding stock, I take it."

"Must be. Yes, those two are bulls, see."

"How can you tell?" Jessica asked. She was teasing, of course. Jessica Starbuck had been raised on a ranch, on one of the largest and finest ranches in Texas. There was little about ranching she hadn't learned early.

"Nothing to it," Ki said with a straight face. "A bull always faces north at sundown."

"By golly! It must be nice to be so well informed."

"Useful, Jessie. There's the house, and here comes an escort."

Ki was pointing up the valley. There, in the deep shadows cast by the surrounding hills stood a grove of cottonwood trees and within the grove an adobe house of fair size for this part of the country with a veranda in the center and two unequal wings. The roof was of red Spanish tile. From the house or near it six riders had emerged, and even at this distance Jessie could see that they were heavily armed.

"He's not taking chances anymore, is he?"

"No. But it seems like locking the barn after the cow is gone."

12

"I only hope we don't look like Apaches."

"Or rustlers," Ki added.

In minutes they were confronted by the Sunset riders. Their leader was a tall, dark eyed, lantern jawed man who looked as if he had just finished dining on lemons and vinegar.

"You folks better just turn right around," he said. "You're riding on private, posted range."

"Mr. Corson is expecting me," Jessie answered a little stiffly. The cowboy was too brusque to suit her.

"Jake, this must be that Starbuck woman the boss was talking about," a second rider put in.

"I am that Starbuck woman," Jessica said, "and Mr. Corson is expecting me."

"You're that one, are you?" the man called Jake asked, peering at her for a long minute. "Rich and pretty too, huh? Well, all right. Who's the Chinee?"

"He is my friend, and he is not Chinese."

"Whatever he is," Jake shrugged indifferently, "the Boss didn't say a word about a Chinee."

"He goes where I go."

"Does he now?" Jake asked, managing to make it a joke. "You got a gun, Chinee?"

"I don't have a weapon with me, no," Ki answered. His voice was even stiffer than Jessie's, but he was holding himself in check, not wishing to waste the time or effort necessary to fight with an ignorant fool like Jake. In fact Ki did have weapons with him, but no firearms, and no weapon that Jake would understand or find menacing. A student of *te* was never unarmed. The side of a hand, the fingertips, an elbow or the foot could be deadly, as deadly as Jake's Colt revolver, but such things went beyond Jake's comprehension.

"All right, I guess you two are harmless," Jake said at

13

last. "Though what the hell you're supposed to do I can't see. I thought the boss had sent for an army or something the way he was talking. Good thing that damn ranger came down anyway."

"Ranger?" Jessie asked.

Jake nodded, spat, and wiped his mouth as they started together toward the ranch house. "Yeah, some Arizona ranger. Etting's his name. Dan Etting—heard of him? Me neither, but he's supposed to be some kind of hotshot." Jake spat again, displaying his scorn. They continued in silence, riding the last mile to the house of Champ Corson. The sky was dark but for a slender crimson pennant above the western hills. In the east there were already stars winking on.

Smoke rose from one of the three stone chimneys of the Corson house and Jessie could smell something cooking. There was a lamp in the window and one across the meadow which seemed to be in a bunkhouse of some sort. The Sunset ranch appeared very prosperous, but there was something of failure, of decay clinging to it.

They reined up in front of the long, twisted hitching rail before the house and swung down. Jessie hadn't realized how tired she actually was until that moment. It felt good to be out of the saddle, but the earth didn't seem too steady underfoot. Through the branches of the huge cottonwoods she looked up to the night sky, then to the house itself.

"Want me to take you in?" Jake asked.

"We can manage," Jessie replied.

Jake nodded, turned his horse, and with his men at his heels, he galloped off through the trees.

"Nice fellow," Ki said.

"I guess they've all got a lot to be edgy about."

"Perhaps. This one—I think he was born that way," Ki said, still watching the dust left behind by Jake and his cowboys. Then smiling, shaking his head, he followed Jessie onto the porch and watched her rap on the gray wooden door.

The woman who opened the door was Mexican, vast and moon faced. She smelled of tamales, spices, and honest toil.

"Yes?" She peered at them with some nervousness, her dark eyes dancing.

"Is Mr. Corson in?"

"Yes." The woman wiped her chubby hands on her apron.

"May we see him, please."

"Yes."

Ki recognized the problem. "She doesn't speak English Jessica," he said, and he proceeded to ask in Spanish if the don wasn't home to Miss Starbuck.

"Oh, yes, yes," the woman said and she moved aside, beckoning them in.

The house was spacious, masculine, nearly unfurnished. There were heavy beams overhead, in one corner by the massive roaring fireplace a huge black leather chair with an open book on it, and on one wall a Navajo blanket. That was very nearly all.

The room seemed empty and the next minute it was filled completely by the vast presence of Champ Corson. His shoulders filled the doorway as he entered, ducking to clear the lintel. He wore a red shirt open at the neck to reveal masses of gray hair on his chest. The rolled up cuffs exposed huge wrists. He was well over sixty, but time had been kind to Champ Corson. His silver-gray hair was thick and wavy, brushed straight back from his forehead. His mustache was gigantic, silver, neatly trimmed. His voice boomed.

"Jessica Starbuck! Damn me! Alex's little baby girl."

Then, although they had never met, the giant rancher threw his arms around Jessie and hugged her like a long lost relative. He was introduced to Ki and shook his hand.

15

"Happy to see you. Sorry it's trouble that brings you visiting." He sighed a little and then broke into a huge grin. "Jessie Starbuck . . . come into the den. What I call the den. I eat there as well, but it's where I spend most of my time so I got to call it something."

With an arm each around Ki and Jessie he led them into an interior room. "We'll eat soon—first you both are damn sure going to get a chance to rest and change though. I got Ramon and others boiling water—that's Elena's boy, you just met Elena at the door. She makes tamales that'll make you want to stay on the Sunset and eat, and eat . . . Sit down over there, Ki. Jessie, find a place."

The den was warm and cozy. A bookcase, apparently homemade, hewn from heavy, dark oak, stood on one wall crammed with every imaginable type of book on every subject under heaven. The furniture was old, heavy. The chairs were of roughly hewn, oiled wood with leather strap backs and bottoms. Jessie sagged into one of these, watching as Champ Corson lit a pipe and waved out the match.

"Everything was in the letter, pretty much," he told them. "Don't hurt to go through it again, I guess." He paused. "Damn glad you came. You know your dad used to buy cattle from me. Ship 'em too. I guess he canned the beef and sold it in his stores, made glue and leather from them cows—wasn't much Alex Starbuck didn't have. But he was a straight man, real straight. Once . . . well, I owe him, let's put it that way though I'll never be able to pay him back now.

"I thought of you first when there was this trouble. There wasn't no one local to turn to. My fault. They all think I'm crooked." He shrugged massively.

"They think you took the cattle?" Ki asked.

"I guess. Let me tell you the whole thing from the start. We got us a large Apache reservation down here. We also

16

got us a considerable number of what we call wild Apaches."

Ki said, "We met a few of them today."

"No, did you? No damage?"

Jessie briefly told Corson about the stagecoach attack.

"Damn," the old man said. "Well, I knew Bourke—can't say it's a great personal loss. Don't know if he had family or not. Wes Gordon was the driver. He was an old-timer around here, a good man made out of wire and leather, I think. Third time the Apaches hit him this year. Third time wasn't a charm for Wes, was it? Good poker player," Corson added irrelevantly.

"This Firesky seems to be the local scourge."

"Yes, he is!" Corson said with some heat. "Killed plenty of people and some of them didn't deserve it." He relit his pipe and puffed at it furiously until his face vanished in a cloud of smoke. "If they'd catch the rascal, that'd be half the problem solved."

"How so?"

"Well, he's a hero to the young bucks, you know. They want to break off the reservation and fight like Firesky. With him if possible."

"That wasn't Firesky who attacked the coach today?" Ki asked.

"Don't know. Doubt it myself. He would've been better organized, had more people. He would've known where the cavalry patrol was before he started any nonsense like that," Corson thought.

"You almost sound as if you admire this Chiricahua Apache," Jessie commented.

"Admire?" Corson cocked his head and gave it some deliberation. "I admire grit and guts and I guess you'd have to say Firesky's got grit. He knows how to fight, when to fight. Maybe I do admire the bastard, but if I saw him this minute, I'd sure hell shoot him dead."

17

"You've crossed paths with him?"

"He's hit me—you'll notice I've got a large crew now. More'n I want really, more'n I can pay, but they'll not run me off this land. I've got twenty-two years invested in it."

"And you've got other troubles."

"Ki, I got every kind of trouble a man my age can have." He smiled and winked at Jessie. "To get back to the start. We've got us an Indian agent here, name of Slattery. Now his job, near as I can tell, is to see if the government can pay him often enough for him to drink himself to death. You never seen the mess he had out there as far as books and distribution of supplies goes."

"Pardon me," Ki interrupted, "may I ask what got you involved in the Indian affairs in the first place?"

"Sure. Slattery."

Ki wanted elaboration and said so. Corson placed his pipe down and explained.

"It's like this. We got trouble building. A thousand Apaches on the Bowie reservation, fenced in, seething, watching Firesky run free and raise hell. The wiser heads— or older heads, I don't know—brought their people in, figuring it was better than being shot down by the army. But the way Slattery manages things, maybe it isn't better."

"The food supplies?"

"That's it on the head. The food supplies don't get here— or Slattery's selling them, I don't know which. All I know is that there's some angry men on that reservation and they'll die by the bullet sooner than they'll starve to death."

"The army . . ."

"Ain't army business. The army and the B.I.A. have been at loggerheads since the B.I.A. was formed. Army has its own solution, you know, and the commander at Bowie is a leading proponent of that solution."

18

"What do you mean? Who is the commander?"

"Major James Neilsen. His idea of handling the problem is to ignore it. If the Indians riot or break out, he'll have them shot down—simple, no?"

"Simple-minded," Ki said in an undertone. Corson heard him.

"That, too."

"What about the Bureau of Indian Affairs people in Washington?" Jessica asked. "Don't they have an interest in looking into this?"

"Possibly. Know how long it takes to get a letter to Washington? Know how long it takes to get someone to *read* it if it comes from a private citizen?"

"Slattery..."

"Slattery wouldn't write a letter if the earth opened up and swallowed all his charges. He stays low, figuring the less noticed he is, the better. Don't bother to ask about the army. It's not army business and Major Neilsen couldn't care less about a bunch of Apaches—sees them as hostiles still, maybe."

"So you got involved."

"I got involved. Out of purely selfish interests."

Jessica said she doubted that and Corson grinned crookedly. "Well, maybe not *purely* selfish, but if the Apaches break off that reservation I'm right in their way. I don't need another war at my age, not if it can be avoided."

"Can it be?" Ki asked incisively.

Corson was thoughtful. "Now—now I don't know, I really don't."

"Evidently you thought so before," Jessica Starbuck put in.

"Yes, I did! Of course. I could see the problem—the Apaches on the reservation were hungry and the food they had been promised wasn't getting there."

"Why?"

"That's the main question, isn't it? I don't know why. I figured it was Slattery's doing. I got him to give me a charter as beef supplier for the reservation. I bought; I was to deliver. That is where my troubles started."

"Please tell us about it once more," Jessie urged. The letter had told it all, but she wanted to hear it from Champ's lips.

"With a government draft in my hand I went to Santa Fe and bought five hundred head of cattle. I took my own expenses out of the money and paid for my hands, but the money was used properly. Contrary to what some people think in Bowie."

"Who?"

"Just about everyone, I guess. People knew I was having some trouble down here meeting my own payroll . . . well, that's getting away from the story again."

"You started west with five hundred steers," Ki prompted.

"Yes. Yes, we started home. A long drive, and a dry one it was, Jessica. We were within two days of Fort Bowie when they hit us one night."

"Who?" Jessica asked Corson. "Who hit you?"

"You got me. To this day I don't know. Indians, comancheros, whites, Firesky . . . could've been moonmen. But they killed. Killed all but two of my hands—Jake and a man named Baldy Reeves—Baldy's dead now himself, trampled by a bad horse."

Jessie and Ki looked at each other. It was bad luck that only Jake survived the raid. Or was it luck?

"So we dragged our butts on home and prepared ourselves for the worst. I got it, all right. Seems I owed the U.S. government beef or cash money. There wasn't much else to do but put up my own cattle. Well, as I told you, that was when they like to broke me. The night before I was

20

going to drive my own stock to the reservation I got hit. We had bunched the cattle at the head of Horn Canyon and damn all if they didn't hit us again."

"Who?"

"That same question again, Jessica. The key question. I don't know. All I know is I lost five more men and another five hundred head of cattle."

"It was on this raid that the name was mentioned?" Ki asked the rancher.

"That was when it happened, yes. Slim Thurber was the hand's name. He died in my arms. He had time to talk before that hoof he took through his ribs killed him. I asked him did he want to have me write a letter home and he said he didn't have no folks. Then he said, 'Champ, I heard them say a name. It was *Laslo*. Laslo, Champ.'"

And it was Laslo who had his name written down in Jessie's black book.

★

Chapter 3

Champ Corson looked older and grayer just now. Reliving the recent tragedies hadn't been easy. Still he was a mountain of a man and he was able to take a deep slow breath and then smile.

"Bad times, Jessie. This Laslo, now, I don't quite understand why he's so important to you. You say he's a part of this bunch of men who killed Alex and your mother?"

"Yes," Jessica answered. "He is one of them—or so I believe. Laslo isn't a common name in this part of the world, is it?"

"No." Corson scratched his head. "You couldn't call that a common name."

"When my father died," Jessie explained, "he left me a black book."

"A black book?"

"It was a compilation of all he had learned about the cartel, which he gradually came to realize had targeted not only the Starbuck empire but America."

"That's a big pill to swallow, Jessie."

"I know it is, but it's true. Ki and I wish it weren't so, but it is. The cartel wants power, wealth, new territory, new markets for their goods; in short the cartel wants to control the world's commerce and in particular the commerce and wealth of America—it seems to believe that America, without the support of European powers, can still be taken as a colony."

Corson laughed out loud. "Absurd!"

"Is it? Once the economy of a country has been taken who then controls that country's fate?" Jessie asked.

Corson, suddenly sober, considered it. "Who, then, is Laslo?" he asked.

"I don't know. To use a military parallel, he seems to be a major general or perhaps lieutenant general in the cartel's hierarchy. Father thought he was right next to the ruling heads, to those who plan strategy and . . . order executions."

"He is in the black book?"

"He is, but there's nothing definite about Laslo in there. Unlike some cartel members who are more or less an open book publicly, Laslo is a shadowy figure," Jessie added.

Corson nodded. "I can see why this interests you, Jessica. These people murdered your parents. But I just don't see a high-ranking man like this Laslo involving himself in a little cattle rustling—little to them, certainly not to me." Corson smiled. "They want to conquer the world, America at least, and they're worried about me and five hundred head of cattle? I don't buy it."

"Buy it," Ki said quietly. Corson looked at him.

"Why so?"

"There's big money and big trouble involved here," Ki

24

explained. "How many reservations are there in the south-west?"

"Why, I don't know, dozens, but..."

"Each one with a large budget, a budget large enough to feed an entire people. Each one with a potential for big trouble. An entire people is being kept confined by government policy. There is anger, resentment, bottled up emotions—they need little to push them to real violence."

"That's true enough here," Corson admitted.

"It's true everywhere in the southwest. These people have been 'tame' for less than a generation. They recall the old ways well enough, and when they get hungry they'll revert to them. Anyone would."

"But they can't win—that's been proven!"

"Has it? Not without a lot of help, modern weapons, for example," Ki said.

"The cartel would...?"

"Why not? What does it matter to them who is killed or which side wins so long as the country is weakened? So we have a two-pronged attack. There is an immense profit to be made by siphoning off Indian supplies; there is a longer range point in doing so, in inducing dissatisfaction with the reservation system."

"I hadn't given it that kind of thought," Corson said. "Yes, I can see that. Maybe it's not so, but I can damn sure see the possibility."

"And that possibility would justify a high-ranking cartel officer."

"Like Laslo?"

"Like Laslo," Ki said.

"Maybe," Corson said, rubbing his temples. "Maybe not. All I know is that the mention of Laslo got you here, and I'm glad for it. Because no matter what or who is sparking this problem, we've got a damn big, damn ugly situation brewing on the reservation at Bowie."

"This whole thing has left you in a poor financial position, hasn't it?" Jessie asked.

"I've been in worse," Corson said. "The money comes and it goes. Your reputation don't. What pains me, Jessica, is having people around here believe that I manipulated things so that I ended up with a pocketful of money."

"The proceeds from the sale of two herds."

"That's it. Maybe it won't save face any for me, but that's why I'm going to try again."

"Again?" Ki asked, his eyes narrowing. What did this man have to try with?

"Yes. I've taken out a mortgage on the place. I'm going to Mexico day after tomorrow and I'll come back with a herd of cattle or die trying—no one knows about this, Jessie, Ki, so keep it under your hats, will you?"

"Or course. But your crew must know," Jessie suggested.

"Them, oh sure, but they won't say anything."

"Jake—is he your foreman?" Ki asked.

Corson grew wary. "Yes . . . ?"

"I just wondered."

"Well, don't waste your time worrying about Jake. He's my man all the way. He's the only one left from the original crowd, the only one who lasted. Some of the boys started taking off. Not Jake. He's my man. He belongs to the Sunrise."

Or so Corson thought. Ki wondered if it were possible that Jake belonged to the cartel. It wasn't fair, perhaps to think that way, basing a good share of it on personal dislike, but it was odd that only Jake had survived. Only Jake.

"Well," Champ Corson said suddenly, his voice recovering its good-natured boom. "Enough is enough. You both have to be trail weary, dusty, and dry. Have yourselves a clean-up and then let's settle down at the table to demolish

26

some of Elena's tamales." He turned toward the door. "Ramon!" he shouted. "Where are you? Damn all! Ramon! Is that water boiling? My friends want a bath."

A shy dark face peered around the corner.

"The bath water is ready," Ramon said.

"Good. Now then Jessie, Ramon will show you your room. Ki, if you'll walk with me down the hallway I'll show you yours. We'll eat in an hour if that gives you time to clean up and rest."

Jessica was led silently away through an arched doorway and down a hall littered with Navajo rugs to an end room.

"Thank you. *Gracias,*" Jessie said, and Ramon, all of eleven, blushed furiously and bowed away.

She watched him go, then opened the heavy door, and went into the room, which was sparsely furnished with a four-poster, bureau, and in the middle of the floor a zinc-plated bathtub filled with steaming water.

"Welcome to paradise," she told herself. Stripping off her skirt and blouse, letting her undergarments rustle softly to the floor, Jessica crossed to the tub and stepped in gingerly. The water was hot, very hot.

Slowly she sank into the water, letting the warmth surround her flesh, enter tired muscles, soothe her. Settling, she closed her eyes, reached for the soap left on a three-legged stool beside the tub and began washing her long legs. She let the sensation of warmth relax her, calm her nerves. Her thighs tingled slightly. Her breasts, weightless in the water bobbed on the surface of the water. Slowly she washed, humming quietly as she did so, not thinking of Firesky or Laslo or the reservation at all.

The door opened and he walked right in.

The intruder had rust colored hair, broad shoulders, narrow waist. He wore two revolvers low on his hips, a bowie knife hanging from the back of his gunbelt. He wore a dusty

27

maroon shirt and black jeans. He whipped off a well used Stetson and threw it down on the floor.

"Son of a bitch," he muttered. Then he turned toward Jessie, his hand going to his holstered right hand gun as he realized abruptly that he wasn't alone in the room.

"Who the hell are you?" he asked. He started forward and then stopped, his eyes feasting on Jessie's lush body. His hand was no longer on the gun butt. "What are you doing here?"

"Just what it looks like—taking a bath. Mind closing the door on your way out? There's a cool breeze."

Jessie's tone was teasing. The tall man suddenly seemed to be nothing but a big gangly kid. He stammered a little and took a half step back.

"This isn't my room. I thought . . . I've only just arrived. Last night . . ."

"You're Dan Etting," Jessie said. "The Arizona ranger."

"That's right." Etting had his composure back. Jessie would have bet he didn't lost it often. There was a boyishness to the man, but he also radiated physical competence. Besides, she liked his smile.

"Happy to meet you," she said, offering him a wet hand that Etting took, held, and then reluctantly let go. "I guess we'll be seeing you at dinner."

"Yes." Etting was backing away now. He snatched up his hat on the way. "I'm really sorry." His eyes said he wasn't that sorry at all.

"It's all right. Please do close the door."

"Yes," he said, "all right." And then he was gone, the door quietly clicking shut behind him. Jessica smiled to herself and then laughed out loud, sinking deeper yet into the tub.

She did like his smile.

Ki wasn't smiling. The rifle had been thrust through his

bedroom window as he prepared for his bath. Instinct or plain chance had caused him to glance into the mirror on the wall and see the slight movement of the light curtains caused by the muzzle.

Leaping to one side, Ki sprang toward the window, but the rifleman took to his heels. Ki was over the sill and into the dark and cold. He crouched naked against the earth, looking right and then left, listening.

There wasn't so much as a sound. Ki frowned. This one was very good. An Apache? Why hadn't he pulled that trigger? True, Ki hadn't given him a good shot, but still most men would have fired if they meant to kill. This one was good. And very patient. He would be back.

Ki searched the area beneath his window, but the ground was hard packed and he could find no tracks. He looked around once more and climbed in the window. His bath was a quick one with his attention still on the window, with his *shuriken* near at hand.

When he emerged from the tub he toweled off and dressed quickly in denim jeans, a pullover cotton shirt, and a well worn leather vest with many pockets in which throwing stars were kept. On his feet he wore cloth slippers. When Ki emerged from the room, he heard voices from the dining room and he went that way, still wary. He didn't particularly like people trying to snipe at him as he bathed.

Jessie had changed to travelling clothes—tight jeans, white silk blouse, denim vest, a wide brown belt with a square buckle. Somehow she looked radiant in the outfit. A ball gown couldn't have improved things.

At the head of an oval table Champ Corson sat with a glass of wine in his hand. Across the table from Jessie sat a young, apparently enthralled man with good lines to his body and a strong jawline. He turned and rose as Ki entered the room, his expression changing perceptibly, becoming more masculine, older.

"Well, there you are, Ki," Champ said jovially. "This is Dan Etting, our ranger."

The two men shook hands. Etting's grip was firm, his palm very callused, surprisingly so. His eyes were blue-gray and they refused to waver as they met Ki's dark eyes.

They sat and ate. And ate. The tamales were as promised, plump with beef and corn, covered with thick salsa. If that wasn't enough Champ offered steaks on the side. Steaks and biscuits dripping with butter and home style honey. After that there was coffee and conversation.

"I can't find a trace of 'em," Dan Etting said. He settled back in his chair a little, holding his coffee cup on his lap with both hands. "Those cattle Champ had taken from his range have to be up in the hills—they can't have been sneaked out of here. You ever try sneaking a herd of cattle? You have to follow the trails because that's where the water's to be found. You have to go where there's grass—especially in this part of the country, but damn me if I can find a trace of those beeves."

"We couldn't either," Champ admitted. "It's kinda humiliating, too. First few days I hired every sorta gun toting man I could find and we set out to get those cattle back. Never found a trace of them."

"Is that what you've been doing?" Jessie asked Etting. "Searching for the cattle. That's the way you mean to approach this?"

"Sure. Like I say, a herd of cattle can't hide like a few men can. They don't climb good and they don't sneak for sour apples. Find the cattle and I'll find the rustlers. Find the cattle and we've got something to quiet down the reservation Apaches. That's the way I'm going to go about it, yes."

"It is hard to believe the herd could have vanished," Ki

30

said. "Is there a hidden canyon or something like that in the hills?"

Corson shrugged. "I would've said no. I thought I knew this country—now I'd have to say there must be. They didn't fly out of here."

"What would they do with them?" Jessie asked. "Given all the time they need?"

"Stolen cattle? South. Into Mexico. Maybe drive them to the coast. They've got a long way to run, but it can be done. A man from Tucson, George Greaves, did it last year."

"What about the Apaches? Firesky. How do they get past them with those cattle. I assume an Apache can eat beef as well as anyone."

"That's a question, isn't it?" Corson said. He shook his head. "Beats me unless they mean to sit it out until Firesky is hung. That could take awhile. Army doesn't seem to be able to find him, let alone catch him."

Jessie fell silent, meditative. "What's that Indian agent's name?" she asked after a while.

"The agent? Slattery."

"Yes. Slattery. I want to see him."

"Slattery? What for?" Champ Corson said, "He might be a lot of things, but Slattery's no cattle thief. He hasn't got the ambition for one thing."

"No, I don't think he is a cattle thief. But I want to talk to him. If the cartel is behind this, as I suspect, they want more than the cattle. They want all the property and money there is. All they can take from the B.I.A. There will be other shortages, big shortages and I want to have a look at his books—if he has any."

"Doubt that," Champ Corson muttered.

"Besides, it isn't going to do any good for me to ride around the hills looking for cattle. If you and Mr. Etting can't find them, I don't see how I can."

"That's probably true. I wish Etting could turn something up, though." Corson turned moody. He took the remainder of his coffee at a swallow and thunked the cup down on the table.

"Things are pretty tight, are they?" Jessie asked.

"That's hardly the word for it. This mortgage isn't going to help. I'm leaving for Mexico but if I lose that herd on the way back—well, I'm sunk completely . . . and so," he added dolefully, "are the people who live in this part of the country, because if we don't get some meat to that reservation sometime soon, somehow, that fuse that Firesky has lit under the young bucks is going to ignite a powder charge like you've never seen. There'll be blood, Jessie. Plenty of blood and when the smoke clears away there won't be much of this country left to see."

That was the plan then—a three-pronged attempt to solve the reservation problem. Etting was determined to find the stolen herd. Champ Corson was equally determined to drive yet another herd up from Mexico. Jessica and Ki were going to go to the reservation itself to see what Slattery had been up to.

"I know it's the cartel," she told Ki privately. "I can feel it now."

"I think so, yes."

"If it is, then they will have been taking every cent they can get their hands on. Not only on this reservation but on every Indian reservation in the southwest—they don't think small."

"No. Jessie, I don't have to remind you to be careful, do I? Not anymore."

"I'm always careful," Jessie said lightly, but Ki didn't return her smile. She thought, *He still feels the need to watch over me; he still, and forever is loyal.* She said aloud, "'Night, Ki. It's been a long day."

Ki debated with himself over it, but finally decided he had to tell her. "There's someone out there who likes to shoot through bedroom windows, Jessie."

She stopped short and turned around to stand peering at him questioningly. "What do you mean? Someone tried to kill you?"

"So it seems."

"Why didn't you say something earlier?" she asked.

"In front of the others? No."

"Why—you can't mean you think Champ was involved! Or Etting?"

"I can't say. I know there are those who think Champ Corson is getting rich stealing Indian beef."

"Ki!"

"I merely point out a possibility no matter how far-fetched. I must also point out that I have never seen this Dan Etting's credentials."

"No," Jessie said. "Maybe it's Elena or her son, Ramon."

"More likely this Jake or some of his crew—I just wanted to mention these points so that you will be careful."

"Why, there wasn't any need at all for all this, Ki," she said. "My room doesn't have a window."

Ki still wasn't smiling. He had a sense of humor but just now it wasn't fully functioning. He watched the woman with the long honey-blond hair walk away from him down the corridor, then shaking his head, he returned to his own room to sleep lightly, very lightly after moving his bed to the opposite side of the room.

Chapter 4

There were a lot of blue uniforms in sight. The sun was hot and white in a pale blue sky, the land copper and white with scattered splashes of palest green as grass roots found moisture or a hunched, wind-tormented cottonwood lifted its head above the surrounding dry brush.

Jessie and Ki were stopped before they reached the reservation proper. A heavy corporal too old for his rank and having the marks of drink on his face stopped them as they passed a disused water tower. Ki noticed two riflemen on the tower. The army was ready for trouble; that was obvious.

"Sorry, Miss. No entry," the corporal said mechanically.

"I want to see the Indian agent, Slattery."

"Sorry, Miss. No entry." The inflection was the same.

Jessie sighed. "How can I get to see Mr. Slattery? Is his office on the reservation? Is he there?"

"You'll need a military pass."

"Yes. And how do I come by a military pass?"

"Fort Bowie, Miss. At headquarters."

If the corporal knew anything else, he wasn't admitting it. The eyes, resigned and bleary, seemed very distant from the job at hand, from Arizona and the Apache troubles.

"Where to?" Ki asked.

"Fort Bowie. Headquarters," Jessica Starbuck said, and it wasn't all that bad an imitation.

They found the orderly room and marched up and in to see a battered private soldier in a torn uniform sitting to one side, head hanging, faced scabbed. Behind the desk was a narrow, toothy first sergeant, behind him on the wall a map of the territory which seemed mostly to be blank spaces, huge empty stretches of yellowing paper between tiny rays of lines which represented sinks and hills, canyons and dry washes.

"Yes, Miss?" the sergeant asked, rising sharply. He was grinning for some reason.

"I'm trying to find Mr. Slattery, the Indian agent," Jessie said.

"Why, he's out on the reservation, I expect, Miss," the sergeant said. The private behind them moaned.

"Yes." Jessie held herself in check. "Apparently I need a pass to go on the reservation."

"That's right, Miss."

Jessica sighed. "I was told to come here for a pass."

"Well, for that, you'd have to see the commanding officer. Major Neilsen."

"Fine. Is he in?" Jessie was tiring of the game.

"He..." the sergeant cast dubious eyes on the door beside him. "He may be."

"Find out, will you," Ki said.

The sergeant was still grinning as if he couldn't help

himself, but he didn't seem to find the prospect of seeing his own commanding officer all that amusing.

"Yes, sir. Please wait," he said, and then, after rapping at the door, he went through, and they heard the muttered word, "civilians."

There was a silence and then the sergeant reappeared. "The major will see you," he said, looking as if he had just been reamed properly. Jessie and Ki went into Major James Neilsen's office. The private in the orderly room moaned again.

Neilsen was not what Jessica had expected. He was crooked—that is, his left eye seemed larger than the right though both were dark brown, sheltered under massively bushy brows. His mouth seemed to twist to one side. His hair, parted sharply just above the ear, ran glossily over a skull that seemed to be congenitally deformed, narrow with odd planes and ridges.

"What is it?" the major snapped. Apparently he wasn't big on civilian relations.

"I need a pass," Jessica said patiently, ignoring the eyes of the major which seemed to have claws, which moved across her breasts, touching nipples greedily, moving down between her thighs to bury themselves there in an imagined paradise. "A pass to enter the reservation."

"Too damned dangerous for a woman."

"With all those soldiers around?"

"The Apaches—you don't know 'em maybe. They're not people."

Ki said he thought they were. The major gave him a glance that indicated he didn't think Orientals were necessarily human either.

"They're ready to explode out there," Neilsen continued. "They're angry and all they need is a target for that anger to attach itself to."

37

"Why are they angry?"

"Why?" Neilsen looked at Jessie as if he thought she had had too much sun.

"Why, I don't know exactly. No food, I guess."

"I guess." Jessica said, "I want to talk to the agent."

"Are you government people?"

"No."

"Can't see how this concerns you."

"It should concern everyone around here, don't you think, Major?"

"It concerns me because it's my job to keep those damned Apaches on the reservation."

"Not to feed them."

"No, Miss. Not the army. Waste of time to feed them anyway. They only multiply."

Jessica Starbuck stared a long while at the major, wondering if it was worthwhile venting her thoughts when her thoughts angered the major. Probably not, she finally decided. Inspiration caused her to say, "We have beef for sale. I'm in the ranching business." Which wasn't precisely true, nor was it false. She owned more cattle than the major had seen or dreamed of, but she had none in a position where they could be brought to Arizona in time to head off the trouble that was building.

The major accepted the tale. Happily. He seemed half afraid that they were spies of some sort from Washington. Cattle, the profit motive, he could understand. In a sketchy hand he wrote a pass quickly and pushed it across the desk.

"Nice man," Ki said outside.

"Life makes people bitter. They find different things to be bitter about."

"Philosophic today?"Ki asked.

"Maybe." It was hot. Jessie looked to the skies. There wasn't a cloud in sight. The soles of her feet were hot. They

38

had wasted all of the morning. "Let's find Slattery and find out what's going on."

They found Slattery, but he wasn't willing to give them any information. He was lying on the floor of his rickety, steaming hot office. He had his eyes wide open, but flies were walking across them. He was very dead.

"At the base of the skull," Ki announced after crouching to search for the killing wound, for certainly Slattery hadn't expired from overindulgence although the office reeked of rotten whiskey. "One thrust. A double edged blade. Very expert."

"The cartel?"

"An Apache does not kill this way. A soldier, a cowhand does not." Ki stood, dusting his hands. Seeing a spot of maroon on his palm he wiped it on his pants. "I think that it was the cartel, yes."

Jessica looked around the room. A fly droned past and batted itself against the filthy bluish window. Someone had done a job on the room. The filing cabinet was emptied, overturned. The desk drawers were scattered across the room. A bottle of ink appeared to have exploded and smeared everything in a ten foot radius.

"We won't find anything here," Ki said. "Not now."

"Let's look anyway. They didn't kill him because of his personal habits."

"No." Ki's expression indicated that they perhaps should have. The body reeked of unwashed flesh, whiskey, tobacco smoke, and sweat.

The search was arduous, profitless. There was enough paperwork, government style, to sink a ship, but none of it seemed relevant to the economics of the reservation—there were no records of supplies ordered, money appropriated, spent, banked. The safe was empty. A nearly crude attempt at framing the Indians lay beside it. A broken turquoise necklace which Jessie kicked aside angrily before sagging into a curved back, wooden swivel chair.

"Well, now what?" she asked.

"We ask those who know what has happened here," Ki answered.

"The Apaches."

"Yes, the Apaches."

"Will they let us talk to them? The army seems to want us to get out and as soon as possible."

"I don't know what the army will let us do," Ki said, "I'm only trying to find a course of investigation. If we cannot . . ."

"Wait a minute!" Jessica Starbuck came to her feet. Hands on hips, she paced the room, the paper on the floor crackling underfoot. "I know what we're going to have to do. What *I* am going to do."

"Yes?" Ki asked cautiously, not liking the tone of Jessie's voice.

"We're short an Indian agent, Ki."

Ki glanced at Slattery's body. He had to agree.

"Well?"

"No, Jessica!"

"Why not? Temporarily? Until they can get someone down here? It's the only way to do this. It will give us access to all the records, to the Apaches themselves, to all avenues of investigation."

"And put you in harm's way."

"That's where we stand now, Ki, where we always stand. Since the day we decided that we would find the killers of my parents, challenge and break the cartel." Her green eyes flashed as she spoke and the resoluteness Ki both admired and feared sparked there.

"You should consider it twice, Jessica."

40

"I have. What else is there to do, Ki? What else if we mean to stop this?"

He didn't have a good answer for her question. He didn't like it, but he had to admit she was right. The Indian agent, whoever he was, was at the heart of the situation. Only he would know where funds were being skimmed; where short goods, rotten goods were being delivered; where the profit was being taken. And only he—she, Jessica Starbuck— could follow the strands of this pilferage and violence to its head.

"Can it be done?" Ki asked, already surrendering to the necessity of her plan.

"Certainly. At least I hope so. Jack Freeman is the deputy B.I.A. secretary. Jack used to do some banking with my father. Some serious banking. It's time to collect a small favor. After all, all I'm asking for is a temporary post."

"There is a telegraph line east—if the message can be routed through to Washington on a priority basis."

"Watch me," Jessie said. The name Starbuck had its own priorities. If Ki had forgotten who owned that telegraph line, he was now reminded. Money, after all, was power.

The corporal who was asked to use the army telegraph to send a message through to Washington at the highest priority looked more than dubious. A little mockery lifted his lips until the first part of the coded message was answered by a stuttering go-ahead from the Santa Fe relay, which cleared all the other traffic from the line and urged the corporal to proceed with the message.

The mockery vanished.

It hadn't returned when in less than an hour—an inconceivably brief time, theory aside—a return message from Washington arrived, sent torridly down the wires as if the world depended on it.

"Is that my message?" Jessica Starbuck asked.

"Yes, Miss. Yes, it is."

He handed it to her and she smiled. Glancing at Ki, she nodded. "Success."

"I hope so," Ki said under his breath. Was it success to place Jessica at the center of this mess, in a position where the last agent had been murdered? Yet it was probably necessary—Ki knew that as well as Jessie did.

"All right, then," Ki said. "You're the Indian agent. What are you going to do to stop this thing?"

But she didn't have an answer. Jessica tucked the telegram of authorization in her blouse and stood, hands on hips, head cocked, watching Ki. "Try," was all she managed to come up with. Try and hope that was enough. It seemed a little doubtful.

The Indian agent's office needed to be cleaned up. Slattery had to be taken away, which he was by three soldiers with a wagon who didn't seem thrilled with the detail. Then the paperwork was collected, the floor scrubbed, the furniture turned upright. Then suddenly there was nothing to do, nowhere to go, no lead and no hint of a solution.

"What now?" Ki asked.

"Back to the fort, Ki. The army must have cattle they could share on a temporary basis. Let's just see if Major Neilsen won't consider that."

Ki looked doubtful. "It's worth a try, I suppose," he said.

They returned to the fort, riding slowly past the army stockpens which didn't seem very full, but neither were they empty. It was enough to give them hope, but the hope didn't last long.

They ran into Lieutenant White just outside of the orderly room door. The young officer looked a little sheepish.

"Good afternoon, Lieutenant," Jessie said.

"You can call me Abel," the officer replied.

42

"All right," Jessie answered, "I will."

Ki pointed out, "Something is troubling *Abel*." White's head jerked around. "Isn't it?"

"It's the major—he has asked me to escort you off the post."

"We want to see him. It's about..."

"He is adamant, I'm afraid. He said to take you off. Now."

"Doesn't he have any interest in solving the reservation unrest? None at all?"

"I couldn't say," White mumbled. "I'm sorry."

Jessie sighed. She supposed there hadn't been much point in trying to talk the officer into sharing his beef supply anyway. Yet it was odd that the major should choose to be so uncooperative.

"I could give you an escort back to the Sunset Ranch," Abel offered.

"Uh-uh," Jessie shook her head. "I'll tell you and you tell the major—as of now I'm the temporary Indian agent. I'll be on the reservation."

"That's absolutely unsafe!" He looked at Ki, "Don't you have any influence? Slattery was murdered out there. The same could happen to you."

"Want to escort us out *there?*" Jessie responded, ignoring all of White's hypotheses. He was right—she could get herself killed—but there wasn't much point in worrying about it.

"I'll take you out," he said glumly.

"Do you know a translator?" Ki asked. He looked at Jessica who nodded her agreement. They would need someone to talk to the Apaches.

"There's Bill Winters, but he's out guiding a patrol. There's an Apache girl, Nati, I think they call her. We can find her wickiup. Jessica,"—he took her hand and she felt the slight pressure of his fingertips—"you don't think you're going to *talk* these Apaches into living peacefully out there, do you?"

"No, I don't," Jessica answered.

"Then what . . . ?"

"We're going to solve the problem."

"Without beef?"

"The army has beef, doesn't it?"

"The major wouldn't share the hoofs and horns," White said, dropping her hand.

"I'll find a way."

"Yes," White said doubtfully. He glanced toward the major's office across the parade ground. "Let's go out to the reservation. I'll show you where Nati is."

They rode silently from the fort past a line of weary, dusty incoming soldiers. Two of the men were wounded; there were three horses without riders. Firesky was still out there, still killing, still impressing the young men on the reservation with his bravado and daring.

Jessie looked to the far hills which were the color and shape of flame. There Dan Etting was searching still for the stolen herd. Was he having any luck, or was he as frustrated as they were at the moment?

The guns brought their heads around. Across the flats came a pinto pony, on his back an Apache boy, whipping the horse for all he was worth. Behind him were three soldiers, all firing.

"Damn it all," Abel White muttered.

"Stop them! He's just a boy," Jessica yelled.

"They've got orders to shoot anyone who tries to break off the reservation."

"Stop it!" Jessie shouted again. White seemed incapable of doing so. He looked bewildered as he shifted his eyes

44

from the fleeing Apache boy to the pursuing soldiers and back.

As they watched, the pinto went down hard, its neck dropping between its legs as it rolled, throwing the boy free. The soldiers were still bearing down on the boy who rose, dazed, and started to hobble away. Ki heeled his horse hard and it leaped forward.

"Don't get in the way," White shouted. He might as well have shouted at the wind. Ki wasn't going to sit there and watch the boy be shot down. Jessie yelled something Ki didn't hear. He heard only the thudding of his horse's hooves, the thunder of the guns.

He raced toward the cavalry patrol, meeting them as they loosed another volley at the Indian boy who leaped for an arroyo, his hair flying.

"Get outta the way," a soldier shouted at Ki, who was now among them. Ki grabbed his rifle, twisted and pulled, and the soldier tumbled from the saddle, shouting in anger as he went down. The man to Ki's right tried to shove his pistol into Ki's face, but Ki chopped the side of his hand against the soldier's neck and the lights in the man's eyes went out as he bounced from the saddle.

Before Ki could reach the third soldier, he had reined up and was following the Indian boy into the arroyo.

"Wait!" Ki leaped from the saddle and darted toward the soldier.

"Get out of my way."

"Leave the boy alone."

The gun came around and Ki turned, leaping into the air to execute a *tobi-geri,* a leaping kick that caught the soldier coming in and sent him staggering back, his rifle dropping free as he clutched his stomach. His face was ashen; his eyes filled with fire. Ki saw the knife appear in his hand

45

as if by magic and he crouched, waiting.

The soldier lunged with the knife, trying to tear Ki's abdomen open with a wild slash. Ki just stepped nimbly aside and gave the soldier a back kick as he stumbled by. He heard an enraged growl issue from the soldier's throat as he continued his turning movement to face the man again.

Beyond the soldier he could now see Jessie and Lieutenant White coming. White yelled something, which might have been an order to stop, but the wind took the shouted command and twisted it so that it was not understandable.

The soldier was breathing heavily, his chest rising and falling.

"I'll teach you to butt in, you goddamn chink," he panted.

"There is no need for this. Hold on for one more minute until your officer arrives."

"No—you won't get off that easy, boy," the soldier swore. Then he lunged again. It was a quick movement, better than the last attempt, but still off balance, awkward. Ki had time to analyze the movement, to find the flaws in it, to wonder at a fighting man who seemed to be able to do little more than pull the trigger of a gun.

Ki himself was a different kind of fighting man. All of his body and everything at hand was a weapon. His muscles, tendons, his very nerves had been trained, tested, prepared for battle. Ki moved sinuously, his body at times giving the appearance of softness, almost of feminine grace. But then it could explode with power and speed, with crushing force. He was like a saber sheathed in velvet. Now he unsheathed the steel that was in him.

As the soldier made his move Ki fell back half a step. His right arm was drawn back, turned up, his left remained before him, parrying the thrust of the knife, using a simple slap to divert the blade. Then as the soldier's knife passed

46

harmlessly, the right hand flashed forward with terrible intensity. Ki struck for the diaphragm using a *nakadate*, a middle-knuckle punch. The soldier never knew what hit him.

His eyes rolled back and he flopped flat on his back to the dusty earth to lie there twitching. He was lucky—Ki could do more than disable with that blow. It would have been easy to kill the man.

White swung down from his bay horse before the animal had stopped running and he rushed to Ki waving his arms wildly.

"What in the hell is happening! What did you do that for, damn it?"

The questions seemed to require no answer. Ki instead started off at a trot toward the arroyo. He saw the boy a hundred yards off, weaving through the willow brush which clotted the bottom of the arroyo, and Ki turned on the speed, his long legs closing the gap between himself and the boy with each stride.

The arroyo began to narrow and turn away to the south. Ki saw the boy look back, saw his eyes go wide as Ki leaped from the bank and landed softly, a few feet behind the Apache who seemed to be ten or eleven.

Ki reached out and grabbed the boy by the back of the white cotton pullover he wore. The boy screamed in rage and he turned and twisted, fighting like a wildcat, clawing at Ki's face, kicking at his groin, none of which had any success against Ki who fended off each angry blow until the Apache boy gave up and sagged in his grip. Then together, Ki still holding his shirt, they started back toward Jessica and Lieutenant White.

His soldiers had gotten to their feet and straggled over, and they stood looking hazily at Ki as he approached them.

"Is he all right?" Jessie asked.

"I think so," Ki told her.

"Little bastard caused enough trouble," one of the soldiers muttered.

"He caused trouble?" Jessica asked. "Why, because he was hungry and he got tired of being locked up? I'd cause trouble too, and plenty of it. You'd likely shoot me down as well."

That, the soldier decided, looking her over, would be pure waste, but he didn't answer. The lieutenant wouldn't have cared for it. Instead the soldiers retrieved their horses and they started north toward the reservation with Jessica Starbuck's first charge in hand.

He was just a boy, but he had had the nerve to break out, the need to. And how long would it be before others broke out, others who were older, who would find weapons, who would kill out of hunger?

Jessie looked at Ki who rode with the boy in front of him. He must have been sharing her thoughts because he nodded and said.

"Soon. It must be done soon."

Chapter 5

The boy was dropped off at his mother's wickiup—only a collection of bent poles with brush interwoven. The woman only stared. She didn't hug the boy or scold him; she didn't speak to the whites. When they left she was still standing there, staring.

"Nati lives over there, near the big oak," White said. "She speaks English very well. She was a missionary girl once, went wild again, and ended up here."

"All right. Thank you," Jessica said.

"That sounds like you're telling me good-bye," White said with an uncertain smile.

"That's right. I don't think it's helpful to have uniforms around if we can help it. I'll talk to the woman—Ki and I."

"I'd like to help..."

"You have," Jessie said and if there was some censure

in her tone, it went over White's head. He turned his horse and slowly rode away. They waited until he had gone then started toward the wickiup which was no poorer, no better than most of the others. A yellow dog lay sleeping in the dust beside the wickiup. It didn't even rise as Ki and Jessie swung down.

They walked to the entranceway which was hung with a rust and purple blanket and called in.

"Nati?"

"Who is?"

"My name is Jéssica Starbuck; I'd like to see you."

"What for?"

The voice was fairly pleasant, but there wasn't a lot of eagerness in it.

"I'm the new Indian agent."

"A woman?"

"That's right. Slattery has been killed as you probably have heard."

"That was good news." She suddenly appeared, pulling back the blanket to peer out into the bright afternoon sun.

She was beautiful. Not just pretty, but strikingly beautiful, and Ki felt his mouth go dry. She had long legs and a narrow nose for an Indian, full petulant lips, clear dark eyes. Her waist was small, her breasts which were hidden behind a white blouse, full, youthfully uptilted.

"I am Nati," she said and she emerged to stand, arms folded beneath her breasts, looking from one to the other. "What tribe are you?" she asked Ki.

"I'm not Indian," he told her. "I am half-American, half-Japanese."

"I heard once of Japan. It is an island."

"Yes," Ki replied without smiling.

"And you are the Indian agent," she said, looking appraisingly at Jessie. "No good. It is too hard a job for you.

50

For anybody," she added after a second thought.

"Maybe. I'm going to try though; that's why we wanted you to act as an interpreter for us."

"Interpreter?" she shrugged. "Why? No one will talk to you."

"We'll see about that, too. Anyway, we mean to straighten out things around here if it's at all possible."

"Sure straighten out everything," Nati said. "Bring food and blankets."

"We're trying to do that, too. I want to explain that to the Indians."

"They won't believe you. We've heard that before," Nati said.

"Don't worry—I won't let anyone starve."

"No? What are you going to do? You know the soldiers have food, blankets, clothing. We have nothing, but they have plenty."

"Maybe we can change that."

"Sure," Nati said a little scornfully.

"You can believe her," Ki said. "You can believe Jessica Starbuck when she tells you something."

"Yes?" She cocked her head. "Can I believe you too, half-this, half-that man?"

"You can believe me," Ki said quietly.

She moved her shoulders slightly in an indefinite gesture and then said brightly, "All right. I will try, too. What else is there to do? What do you want to learn?"

"First of all I want to find out who's taken the beef. You say you are also short blankets and clothing?"

"We are short of everything. Medicine, food, tools. Nothing comes. Nothing we were promised. We were each supposed to have a blanket, each family was supposed to have a home. We were supposed to have farm tools, horses, knives, pots, and pans..."

51

"You haven't gotten any of this?"

"Nothing. Nothing at all."

"It adds up to quite an amount of money, doesn't it, Jessie?"

"Enough to make it worthwhile—especially if they can stir up revolution while they're making a profit."

"Who?" Nati asked, but there wasn't time to explain the cartel to her. It would have been meaningless anyway. The people here cared about their bellies, not international power politics, economic plots, and subversion.

"I want to know if anyone saw the man who killed Slattery. Someone must have. A white man couldn't have slipped onto the reservation, done the deed, and slipped away again."

"You think it was a white man!" Nati said in disbelief.

"Yes, I do."

"No one else will. If I could have killed him..." her voice trailed off into bitter silence.

"We have reasons for believing a white man killed Slattery. To cover up the theft of government goods. We need to find out if anyone saw the killer."

"All right." Nati nodded. "I will help you to find out."

Jessica said decidedly, "There's really no sense in both of us interviewing the Indians, Ki. If you want to go with Nati..."

"And you?"

"I want to go over the agency building again. A lot of papers have been stolen or destroyed, obviously, but it seems to me that Slattery, anyone involved in something like this, would keep a little something back to try to hold over the heads of his associates."

"A little blackmail?"

"Maybe. Maybe just a little protection. Anyway, I'm going to go through the building again and then I'm going to get on the telegraph and see if we can't get someone moving on these supplies. If I have to, I'll have the local bank wired and I'll buy supplies myself locally."

Nati looked at the determined blond woman wonderingly. "Does she mean it?" she asked Ki after they had split up, Jessie returning to the agency building.

"She means it. She'll get food to this reservation somehow."

"To keep a war from starting."

"Because people are hungry," Ki told her. "Come now, let's do our best to help out."

"By finding this killer?"

"Yes. Because the killer, whoever he is, is very likely working for the people who took your cattle and other supplies."

"Perhaps. Ki, this will not be easy," Nati said.

"We'll try."

Trying wasn't enough. It wasn't only difficult; it was impossible to get anyone to talk. They entered wickiups or talked to people crouching in the late shade beneath the trees. Nati cajoled, smiled, teased, begged but there was no response at all from those who lived near the agency building. Stoic, expressionless dark faces stared back with silent defiance. Perhaps no one had seen the killer. Perhaps they thought that whoever it was, he had done them a favor by killing the ineffective agent.

It was sunset before Ki gave it up. There was no one left to talk to, nowhere left to go.

"And so I have failed. Now I will go."

"Don't make that sound so final."

Nati was leaning against a twisted oak tree. Behind her the sky was fire and gold. She had her clasped hands before her.

"It is final, is it not?" she asked.

"No, not if I know Jessica. She won't be ready to give

53

up yet. We'll still need someone to talk to the Apaches for us."

"Yes." She smiled and then turned her eyes down. "You, Ki? Are you through with me."

"I don't understand you," Ki replied. Or did he? The sky was going dark. The air was still warm, a faint breeze stirring the leaves of the oak. Her hand reached out and touched his arm.

"Maybe you are not through with me," Nati said and Ki stepped to her, drawing her body against his with one arm slung around her slender waist. She sagged against him and her lips parted as her head lolled back. Her eyes danced with cool fire, and even in that poor light Ki could read a hunger that matched his own.

"I have wanted you since I first saw you."

"Then take me," Nati said, and her smile became a serious thing, a challenge, a question. She let Ki kiss her and then, taking his hand, she said, "I know a place."

She led him then through the trees as sundown swept across the sky like wildfire.

Beyond the trees was a surprisingly wide canyon, opening up in the dark earth. Nati guided Ki surely down a narrow trail to the sandy bottom where with surprise Ki saw the narrowest of rivers, a pencil thin rill, darkly colored by the sunset, weaving its way southward through the brush which crowded the bottom of the canyon.

"Here," Nati said and they ducked low, turned right, and then found themselves in a thicket, a hidden place where grass, short and springy, covered the ground.

It was still and warm. Frogs grumped in the willows. Crickets chirped frantically beyond the thicket and the first stars were erupting in the evening sky.

Nati turned, removed her blouse, and stepped from her skirt. She wore nothing underneath. She was smiling as she came to Ki who felt his loins stir, his manhood rising. Nati sagged against him, her mouth twisting against his, her tongue following Ki's lips as his hands rested on her shoulders then sank to run across her narrow waist, her full, solid buttocks.

"I will help you; do you need help?" Nati asked as her hands went to his crotch, her fingers working almost frantically at the buttons to his jeans.

He didn't need any help at all, but he wasn't going to refuse it either. He let his own hands run up her inner thighs, feeling her shudder, enjoying the sleekness of her legs, the strength that lay beneath the smooth coppery flesh. His fingers probed for and found her soft cleft with its flourishing bush as his own jeans opened wide and he sprang free to be encircled by Nati's hand.

"Come," she said softly and she led him back a way slumping to the earth, keeping his hand in hers as she lay back, smiling up at him with starlit eyes.

Ki disentangled himself long enough to yank his shirt off and kick off his shoes. Then he went to her, kissing her ankle, her knee, her inner thigh as Nati's hand rested on his head.

She was sleek and lithe and beautiful by starlight. Her pulse was strong, rapid beneath Ki's lips. She lay with her hair spread across the earth, her lips parted, her legs lifting, knees parting as she pulled Ki to her.

He kissed her mouth, her throat, and then her breasts, cupping them in his hands as he kissed one nipple and then the other. They were taut, dark, long, magical, and Ki feasted on them for a long while, his tongue and then his teeth teasing them as Nati moaned softly deep in her throat, as she reached for and found his shaft which she tugged at eagerly.

Ki shifted positions. Kneeling between her legs he spread

55

her uplifted knees still wider and waited as Nati prepared herself.

Using the head of his erection, she rubbed herself, teasing the soft inner flesh, bringing forth fluids. She toyed with him until she could no longer stand it, until Ki himself was teased beyond endurance, and then she slipped the head of it inside, only the head and she lay there looking up at him, panting, her beautiful breasts rising and falling as Ki knelt over her.

Her fingers went between his legs and cupped his heavy sack. She tugged him in a little, half an inch, her warmth surrounding him. Ki felt her shudder.

He bent low once, kissed her abdomen, and then raised himself again, the motion causing him to nudge Nati slightly, to ease himself inside a little farther. Now she clutched at his shaft, her fingers nervous, needful and with a groan of surrender she lifted her hips and thrust her pelvis against him, taking him in slowly, deeply, grabbing at his arms, his shoulders, dragging him down to meet her suddenly animated, writhing body.

Ki was locked in her arms, kissing her throat, eyes, lips, feeling her warm breath against his ear as she pitched and swayed against him, her pelvis slapping at his, her body going liquid and slack as she threw her legs around him, her heels nudging his buttocks, directing his cadence which grew faster, more intent until with a muffled cry Nati found a hard, quick climax which caused her body to tremble with wave after wave of sensation.

Ki had been holding himself back only with difficulty. She was warm and close and she wanted him. Her body was demanding and what it demanded Ki now gave her as his own intense orgasm drained his loins with a sudden rush which lingered as a series of small spasms, which seemed to match the beating of Nati's heart.

She stroked his back and they lay in silence, feeling the warmth of their bodies, the gentle night breeze, and listening to the night creatures.

Until Ki heard something that was not of nature, that did not belong to the soft night, and he came instantly to his feet, leaving Nati to gasp with surprise. Ki moved to his clothing and withdrew two *shuriken* from his pockets.

Nati started to say something, her lips parting questioningly, but Ki put a finger to his lips, signaling for silence.

There was something moving in the brush beyond the clearing, and although the sounds it made were soft and indistinct, Ki knew. He knew it was a man.

The assassin? The man who had killed Slattery and tried to kill Ki at Corson's ranch? Or only a hunter, a curious kid.

Then Ki heard no more. He no longer sensed danger. But his mind was uneasy. He dressed hurriedly as Nati watched him with disappointment.

"What was it?" she asked, still sitting naked on the earth, her arms braced behind him.

"Someone was watching."

"I heard nothing."

"Nevertheless, someone was there," Ki assured her.

"Not..." Her hands went to her lips. Her eyes were wider and now she reached for her clothing, dressing quickly.

"Not who?" Ki demanded.

"Nothing. No one."

Ki took her shoulders. She had her skirt on, but her blouse was clenched in one hand, hanging between them as Ki squeezed her shoulders a little more sharply.

"Who? I have to know."

"I don't know who it was." Her eyes slid away from Ki's.

"You have an idea."

She hesitated for a long while and then looked into his eyes again. "There is a man. He thinks I want to marry him ... If it was he ..."

"What's his name?"

"Ka-te-Ana. Skull, he is called."

"Do you think it could have been him?"

She shrugged and Ki looked to the skies. He asked her, "What does he look like? How will I know if I see him."

"It will be easy," she said. "There has never been an Apache so big."

"Bigger than I am."

"Much bigger," she said. "Mangas Coloradas is six feet and a half tall. I have seen Skull beside him. He was a head taller."

"What would he do—Skull—if he was there, if he saw us, Nati? Is he the kind to kill?"

"He is Apache," she shrugged. "If it was Skull in the bushes, he will kill."

There wasn't much point in worrying about it, Ki decided. If Skull came around, then it would be decided. He smiled at the healthy, lusty woman before him and kissed her neck, holding her for a moment.

"You are not angry?" Nati asked.

"How could I be angry when you have given yourself for my pleasure."

"Then it was good?" she asked, brightening.

"It was very good ... Nati, this Skull wouldn't hurt you, would he?"

"No, he would not dare," she said with some passion and much certainty.

"All right, then, we won't worry about Skull. Let him sulk for a while."

Nati finished dressing, pulling her blouse over her head,

putting her moccasins on, tying her hair back loosely with a rawhide string.

"I am sorry we accomplished so little tonight," she said as they started back through the trees.

"We accomplished much," Ki said, slipping his hand around to cup her breast. She laughed softly and kissed him.

"Yes, but nothing for the good of the people."

Ki grew serious again. No, nothing had been accomplished for those who were hungry, for those who wanted to be away from the reservation badly enough to risk getting shot down.

"Perhaps Jessica has found something." Or Dan Etting. Perhaps Champ Corson would bring that herd up from Mexico in time to help. Ki felt desolate for a moment, frustrated knowing he was contributing nothing at present. Nothing but romantic entanglements.

He kissed Nati good night and started walking toward the Indian agent's office where a lamp still burned. Across the camp a dog yapped at the night spooks and a child cried—with hunger? Now and then Ki passed groups of men, Apache warriors, standing together, talking in low voices. He could feel it now, feel the tension in the air, feel the growing urge to strike back blindly at any target. If the cartel had intended to stir up unrest on the reservations, to divert and challenge the United States army, they were succeeding quite well.

He reached the little white house, went up the steps, and opened the door to find Jessica standing in the midst of chaos.

Papers were still strewn everywhere. They seemed to be shifted around, however, as if a breeze had entered the office and redistributed the mass of documents Slattery had left behind.

Jessie looked up hopefully to Ki who shook his head. "I'm sorry. There was no progress at all. I don't know if anyone saw anything or not, Jessica, but I know this—they aren't going to tell us without good reason."

"Well, that's more or less what we expected," she said with a small sigh. She was looking around her at the ravaged office.

"And you, I take it, had no luck?" Ki crouched, picked up a voucher three years old, tossed it away, and waited for an answer.

"Nothing. I haven't torn up the floorboards yet, but outside of that I'm convinced that if there was anything here it was removed after Slattery was murdered."

Ki nodded. He moved around the room seeing the remains of disorganization. There *had* to be something. Slattery had handled thousands of dollars in bank drafts, in goods. He had to have had a hiding place for his private papers, a place to hide his money . . .

Ki stopped. He was before the fireplace and now he stood staring at the ash which remained there. It was layered ash as if books had been burned.

"What is it, Ki?"

He didn't answer. Crouching, he reached for the black iron poker beside the fireplace and began to prod the ash. In a moment he had found a corner of yellow paper, unburned.

Ki took it from beneath the ashes and gingerly handed it to Jessica Starbuck, who even with the soot and discoloration could plainly read the word that a shaking, slanting hand had written there.

"Laslo."

Chapter 6

Jessie and Ki dived into the ashes and half an hour later they were covered with the stuff. There was a smudge on Jessica's nose, one on Ki's forehead. Both of them had black hands. The search had yielded little besides the smudges.

"It's not much, is it?" Jessie said as they placed the few fragments of unburned paper on the desk where Slattery had done his work—if in fact he had ever done any.

"No, it isn't much at all." Ki shook his head heavily. "Laslo" they understood, and in a way it confirmed their theory about what was happening on the reservation, proved that the cartel was involved somehow. But it didn't move the investigation forward a bit.

"Blnkts. One thous . . ." was all that was written on another fragment. A thousand blankets they assumed, blankets meant for the Indians. Blankets that had gone . . . gone where?

"I don't understand this one. What is 'Dorchester'?" Ki asked. "A name? A town somewhere?"

"I don't know." Jessie looked exhausted. "We can ask around. Maybe it's someone local." She suddenly reached out and scattered the charred fragments of paper. The frustration was reaching a high level.

"You need to rest, Jessica," Ki said gently.

"I know it. It's just that the feeling is on me that if we don't do something—us, you and me—and do it soon, the whole thing's going to cave in. I went out for a while today. I saw their faces, saw their eyes. It's a smoldering fire out there and all Major Neilsen is able to think of doing is to shoot anyone who wants out of a bad situation."

"Yes. But there is nothing more we can do tonight, Jessica."

"No, you're right. I know it," she said, poking at her hair nervously. Then she relaxed a little, smiled, and said, "Let's get some sleep and try again in the morning."

That, too, was easier said than done. Jessie Starbuck crawled into Slattery's old bed after turning the straw mattress and throwing his blankets away—Slattery had not been a clean man. Ki curled up on the floor near the fireplace and managed to doze by putting his mind on another plane, by letting his spirit self wander distant gardens where shrubs and flowers were brought to bloom by magical gardeners who splashed the world with lilac blossoms and with crimson and pink roses and the air filled with their sweetness.

Jessica wasn't able to play such tricks on her mind, not on this night. She tossed and turned on the bare bed. It was warm; the mattress uncomfortable. The door between the bedroom and the office was closed and the breeze from the open, starlit window seemed not to touch her.

She rose, rubbed her arm nervously, angrily removed the rest of her clothing, and lay down again on the bed to half-sleep only. She awakened sharply at times, concern and useless, crazy ideas prodding her weary mind.

It was three in the morning before she finally fell into an exhausted sleep, lying on her stomach, her arm dangling to the floor. The breeze was cooler now.

She did not see, but sensed the moving thing which briefly blocked out the stars in the window frame and then slipped to the floor.

She awakened again and rolled over just as the shadow reached her bed. She started to cry out but did not. He had stopped. It was a man, a tall man, and in his upraised hand was a long knife. He had raised it, but he did not drive it down at Jessie's breast.

Now he lowered it slowly and came half a step nearer, his hand, not his knife, finding her smooth body, running over her full breasts, across her abdomen.

Still Jessie did not cry out, fight back, try to run. There was something electric about this man's touch, a magnetism beyond definition, something that leaped at her from out of the darkness. His hand fell away and he stepped back.

Now she could see that he was an Indian, an Apache, and now, too, she could see that he was smiling. He put his knife away then and moved with two catlike strides to the window. He threw his leg over, paused, and looked back at Jessie who was sitting up now, her hair loose around her shoulders, and then he was gone, leaving Jessica Starbuck to feel just a little colder, a little shaken; but when she lay down, sleep came easily and she found herself wandering through a warm and sensuous dream with a faceless man.

The pounding at the door brought Jessie to her feet. The sun was glaring through the window and she squinted against it as she hurriedly dressed, hearing Ki mutter something in annoyance.

After she finished buckling her belt, Ki opened the door

and in it was a very excited Lieutenant Abel White. Behind him was a full platoon of cavalry, milling, looking grave and intent.

". . . was seen by a Zuni scout sometime after three," White shouted.

"I see." Ki was calm, but White refused to be influenced by anything so rational as Ki's serenity. Both men turned toward Jessie as she approached.

"You see, I told you she was all right."

"Thank God. I had to see for myself," White said with vast relief.

"What's going on?" Jessie asked.

"What's going on!" White repeated with a little more intensity. "Firesky."

"Firesky what?" Jessie asked.

"He was seen last night. Here. On the reservation," White explained.

"Last night?"

"Yes. Three or four in the morning. A Zuni scout who had been . . . ah . . . visiting an Apache woman was leaving and returning to his own camp at the army post. He saw Firesky."

"Here? Why?"

"I don't know. Miss Starbuck, he was seen *here*. At the agency building."

"Impossible," Ki said.

"Crawling in your window . . ." White said with some reluctance.

"Yes? This Zuni scout, does he drink trade whiskey?" Jessie asked.

"What do you mean? Oh . . ."

"What took him so long to get the report to you," Ki wanted to know, "if this happened at three this morning?"

"He was attacked. By one of Firesky's lieutenants, he thinks. Knocked unconscious. He only came around an hour ago and dragged himself to the post."

"You didn't say if he drank."

"If he . . . I don't know, I suppose so, yes. What are you suggesting?" White demanded.

"Just this—if Firesky was here, why would he climb in my window and then crawl out without hurting me, without taking me hostage? Just to watch me sleep? I think this scout got drunk, fell down, and knocked his head, Lieutenant. I think he dreamed he saw Firesky. The Chiricahua must be on everyone's mind. It can affect dreams."

White looked doubtful; still he couldn't understand himself what Firesky would have been doing there on the reservation, why—if he had come—he would leave without having left his mark?

"As long as everything's all right here," he said at last.

"It is."

The officer nodded. He looked around, still dubious. "Sergeant! Let's get moving. South he'll be riding if it was Firesky and not some drunken delusion of Roundback's."

Then with a salute White was gone, swinging into the saddle of his bay, leading his men off across the reservation through a storm of dust and a hail of rocks thrown by young Apaches.

Ki stood at the door for a long while, staring after the soldiers. Then he turned and asked, "Well?"

"Well what?" Jessie teased.

"What did you fail to tell the lieutenant?"

She didn't answer immediately. She had her back to Ki when she said musingly, "Firesky."

"Then he was here?" Ki asked with some anxiety. There was some disbelief mixed with his emotions. There were

65

very few men who could enter a window and cross a floor without awaking Ki. If Firesky had done that, he was very good, very deadly.

"Someone was here," Jessica said at last. "This morning before the soldiers came I woke briefly, thinking about it. I decided it was all a dream—apparently it wasn't a dream at all."

"But why?—and what did he want?—"

"And who?" Jessie suggested.

"I don't understand you."

"Maybe Firesky had ideas of retribution in mind. He had come here with a purpose in mind. The only purpose there could have been—from what I saw of his manner and the knife in his hand—was to kill Slattery."

"It could be."

"It must be. He wouldn't have any way of knowing that Slattery had already been murdered. He had come to do that job—and instead he found me in bed."

"A pleasant surprise for Firesky," Ki muttered. "Why would he kill Slattery."

"The agent was shortchanging the reservation Indians," Jessie answered.

"But Firesky is a 'wild' Indian; what does he care?"

"Apparently the man does care."

"It seems logical," Ki admitted. "I don't know. What kind of man is he?"

To his astonishment Jessica just smiled. The knock at the door ended the conversation. It was Nati, her eyes wide with emotion. She entered cautiously as if fearing someone might toss her out. She spared a single soft glance for Ki, which didn't elude Jessica, and then said breathlessly, "He was here they tell me!"

"Firesky? Yes. We think so."

"What did he do? What did he say?"

Nati hung on each word of Jessica's reply, although there wasn't a lot to tell. He hadn't done much, said a thing— not with words. It was obvious that to Nati Firesky was a man of legend, of great stature. The reservation Indians all seemed to shelter a hope now that the great Chiricahua would one day save them, take them from under the nose of the army and lead them to some distant and undefined paradise.

"The soldiers went after him," Ki said.

"They will not catch him. Firesky is a ghost, a shadow, a desert wind."

"You know him?" Jessica asked. Nati turned her eyes down and answered.

"No, not really."

"He had a good lead," Ki said.

Nati latched onto that thought. "Yes. They will never catch him!"

"Nati," Jessica said, "we found some papers in the fire-place here. Papers someone had tried to burn. On one of them was the word 'Dorchester'. Do you have any idea who that is?"

"Dorchester, yes," she said matter of factly. Jessie felt her hopes rise.

"Tell us then, please. Who?"

"The man in town. The trader," the Apache woman answered.

"A trader?"

"A storekeeper, you know. Sometimes he is allowed to come out here and then if anyone has trapped for furs or found turquoise or silver, if anyone has caught many fish, Dorchester will trade with them for a knife or a blanket."

"Trades back a few of the goods the reservation was already supposed to have . . . and makes a greater profit yet." Jessica was incensed.

"Easy," Ki cautioned. "I think you are probably right, but guessing will do us no good."

"What will, then?"

"Visiting Dorchester, I hope."

"It's the only way. Also, I want to go by Fort Bowie and wire for funds, see about getting Starbuck cattle here on the chance that there may somehow be time."

"That," Nati told them, "will not be possible. Didn't the soldiers tell you? Firesky has cut the telegraph wires."

"Damn," Jessie said, "that's not very helpful."

"He couldn't have known. He's just fighting his war the was he always has," Ki replied.

"I guess you're right. Anyway, we can't worry about it now. It just seems that we keep coming up a little short, Ki." She turned to Nati, "Will you *please* try again to talk to anyone around here who might have seen the man who killed Slattery. Perhaps if Ki and I aren't around they will tell you what they saw—if anything."

"I do not think so," Nati answered.

"It's important, very important. They must be made to understand that. The authorities will still believe that an Apache killed Slattery and we have to prove otherwise— there may be retributions. Try to tell them that the man who killed the agent is involved with the thieves who have taken their cattle."

"Slattery," Nati said, "he is the one who stole the cattle."

"Yes, but he had help, lots of help. Please, Nati." Jessie took her shoulders. "Try to get them to open up."

"I will try," she said. She added, "But it will do no good."

"Just try, please."

Nati agreed, but she didn't reflect much confidence in the scheme. She said her good-byes and went out the door into the bright sunlight. It was still early and already hot. The air was dry. The wind was twisting across the reser-

68

vation, drifting the oak leaves. Jessica snatched up her hat and nodded. They started out the door and down the steps, hoping that something at Dorchester's store would put them on the right track. So far they hadn't been running into good luck.

It wasn't due to improve real quick.

As Ki stepped out on the sunlit porch, a massive Apache hurled his body at him. Ki was slammed back and they smashed through the porch railing and to the ground where Ki lay stunned. The big man—Ki thought it was Skull, had to be Skull—stepped back and waited for Ki to rise.

His English, if that was what it was, was awful, but Jessie caught the words, "Kill" and "Nati" distinctly.

Who Skull was she didn't know, but she hadn't run across a more physically intimidating man in a long, long while. His shoulders seemed as wide as two spread arms, his wrists as thick as Jessie's calves. His neck was a column of bronze. His eyes were small, black, murderous. His huge chest heaved with emotion as Ki got groggily to his feet, obviously stunned.

"Now I will kill," Skull said and he tried it.

He leaped at Ki again, and Ki, groggy still, stunned, backed away and only reflexively blocked a kick with his crossed wrists and spun to lash out with a side-kick which had little force behind it.

Skull grunted, and perhaps inspired by the other Apaches who had come running to watch the battle, he produced a nasty looking knife from somewhere. He showed it to Ki as if offering it for sale, then slashing up from down below he tried to rip his throat out with it.

Ki's reflexes again held him in good stead. Though his mind was reeling still from the crush of the giant's body, his body, trained to respond automatically, instantly did so.

Ki blocked the knife's upward motion with a *gedanbarai*,

a downward block which half-turned Skull with its force. Under normal circumstances he would have completely turned him.

Now his head was clearing and Ki assumed a stance from out of a spin, waiting for Skull, who came in again, to meet the body crushing force of a *yonhon-nukite* blow. It was enough to kill a lesser man, but Skull was vast and even Ki's skills were not going to put him away easily.

The Apache's knife was gone, but he had his bare hands, hands which they said had bested a grizzly bear in the Sierra Madres, hands which could twist an inch-thick iron bar or crush a normal man's head.

He intended to do something like that now to Ki, but he had waited too long. His first unsuspected attack had driven Ki to the earth and robbed his lungs of air, stunned his brain, but the big man's skills were no match for Ki's and now he had to pay the price.

Skull grabbed at Ki, missed as the samurai ducked away, and took an elbow in the diaphragm. Skull *oofed* and backed away, blinking with astonishment. He came in again. Ki was waiting.

The giant roared as he went in, a battle cry which had horrified many men, which had rung in their ears as they died, but Ki didn't intend to die. He ducked and side-kicked again, his heel smashing into Skull's nose, flooding the Apache giant's face with blood, driving two teeth back and in, tearing them from their roots.

Skull backed away, turned his head, and spat. He didn't care about the teeth. He had others. What he cared about was losing face in front of the others, and that could be happening. The Apaches who had gathered to watch Skull maul the stranger were now being treated to another kind of show.

Skull's size and deadly intent were overmatched by pure

skill, by the years of training under the masters of *te*. Ki blocked an overhanded blow with ease, turned, side-kicked, kicked again and backed into his dragon stance.

Skull learned slowly. He pressed ahead, trying to grab at Ki, to pull him into his huge arms, to tear his head off. He achieved nothing. It was like trying to capture smoke.

An elbow to the solar plexus again deprived the big Apache of his breath and he backed away, trying to kick at Ki's kneecap, to break it and cripple the leg, but Ki leaped over the effort and again crouched, waiting.

Skull staggered forward, his bloodlust waning. Something had gone wrong, but what? This narrowly built foreigner had the reflexes of a cougar, the sudden strength of one. His hands struck like rattlesnakes, darting here and there, inflicting sharp pain, but pain which seemed to be deliberately softened as if the man did not wish to cripple, to kill, but only to warn.

That made no sense to Skull. A fight was to be won. To kill was to win. He came in again, feeling empty, as if the blows of the foreigner had sapped him of his will, of his power, and of his very soul.

Still Skull would fight, and if he could, he would kill. He found his knife on the ground, gleaming in the bright sunlight, and the Apache's own eyes gleamed as he picked it up.

As Skull came in, circling slightly, Ki seemed to shake his head as if with sadness. When Ki lashed out this time it was with the speed of lightning, with sudden, almost inconceivable motion.

A hand struck, then the other, both together, a knuckle inflicting pain beyond belief. The knife was chopped from Skull's hand as a nerve in his wrist was deadened.

Then that same wrist was gripped, seemingly with only fingertips which lightly touched his flesh, and Skull found

71

himself flying across the foreigner's shoulder to land flat on his back on the hard earth beneath the hot white sun.

He lay there, unmoving. He thought he could have gotten up and again attacked the stranger who had been with Nati, but it just didn't seem worth it. The man would simply use his magic to throw Skull again, to defeat him in front of his people, to humiliate him. And so Skull lay still, closing his eyes against the glare of the hot sun, falling off to a stunned and peaceful sleep.

"You're all right?" Jessie asked Ki.

"Yes." Ki looked at the gathered Apaches with some trepidation. "Nati, will they let us through?"

"It was a fair fight," the woman answered. "They will not interfere."

"Good. Jessica, it is time to go now, time to find this man Dorchester . . . or Laslo."

"Yes," Jessica answered. It was time, it was past time so the hungry eyes, the angry eyes revealed as Ki, Nati, and Jessie eased through the gathered Apaches and started toward Bowie.

Chapter 7

Bowie lay still beneath a torpid noonday sun when Ki and Jessica Starbuck rode in some time later. There was activity at the fort, but they couldn't see exactly what the nature of it was. Probably, they decided, another attempt to track down the elusive Firesky. It wouldn't have made Major Neilsen very happy to know that the Chiricahua could move around the fort and reservation with impunity. Knowing Neilsen, Jessie and Ki realized he would be enraged.

The little town which had grown up in the shadows of the fort was a place where local Indians, Americans, and Mexicans clustered together for protection from the Apaches on the desert. There was nothing much to support it but need.

Five cantinas lined the dusty, twisting main street, four of them made from adobe blocks, the last of gray, apparently scavenged lumber. A portion of the front porch seemed to have been made from the planks of a wagon bed.

There was a land office—closed up; a boarding house— empty; and the general store with a freshly painted green sign hanging from the eaves—Dorchester's.

Jessica swung down from her horse, tugged her jeans down, and dusted off as Ki hitched up. Then they started up the plank steps and into the building.

The interior was rich with the smells of leather, salt pork, new jeans, pickles, blankets, and bay rum. There was a single customer, an old Mexican lady in black with a lace mantilla on her head, standing with a bolt of cloth in her hands and looking toward the back room beyond the low, scarred, wooden counter.

"What is it?" Ki asked.

"Where is he? Where is help when you want it? Where is Dorchester?"

"How long have you been waiting?"

"Fifteen minutes. Half an hour. Where is he? Where is help when you want it?"

Ki and Jessie exchanged a look that conveyed much. Ki started toward the back door as Jessica escorted the woman and her purchase toward the front, assuring her that she would give the money to Dorchester.

Not that it would do Dorchester any good.

He was a bald, cherubic man with pale blue eyes and stubby little pink fingers like sausages. His tongue protruded from his mouth, black and swollen. He lay on the floor of his office with a noose of bailing wire around his throat.

Ki was crouched over him when Jessie returned.

"Is it him?" she asked.

"That's what the papers in his wallet say."

"Laslo is covering his tracks."

"He knows we are looking." Ki stood, dusting off his

74

hands. "The only way he can cover his tracks permanently is to eliminate us as well."

"What do we do now?"

"I wish I knew. First of all, let us leave. I don't want to be questioned about this, do you?"

"No, I..." Jessie's reply was interrupted by the unmistakable, chilling sound of gunfire. It was distant, brief. A dozen shots fired rapidly and then silence. They stood looking toward the reservation beyond the walls, listening for more shots which never came.

Outside, people had come into the streets, some from the cantinas with beers or whiskey glasses in hand. Jessie could hear some of the speculation. "Firesky... tried to attack the fort... break off the reservation... coming right for town."

Jessie and Ki were into their saddles and riding. The sky was blue; the day perfectly still, dry. There seemed to be no activity at the fort. The flag still fluttered lethargically in a soft breeze. The sentries walked their posts. Then Ki pointed and Jessie, too, saw the trouble.

To the west of the post was the cavalry unit's stockyard where the beef to feed the soldiers was kept. Two dozen soldiers were milling around. Two officers sitting on their horses watched. The cattle moved restlessly in their pen, horns clacking together, their eyes wide. On the ground lay three dead Indians.

Jessie muttered something bitter and unintelligible. They heeled their horses and raced toward the scene of the shooting, recognizing Major James Neilsen now and beside him Lt. Abel White. The soldiers were searching through the pens, moving the cattle aside, presumably looking for more Indians—alive or dead.

"Damn it all!" Jessica Starbuck said loudly, startling the major. "What is happening here?"

"What business is it of yours?" the major asked. The young lieutenant was giving Jessie a pained, sympathetic glance. She ignored it.

"I'm the Indian agent here; that's what business it is of mine," Jessie said, losing her temper completely. It didn't faze the major a bit.

"Then I suggest you keep your charges on the reservation and out of my stockyard."

"I would if I had anything to feed them," Jessie shot back. "I would think that a man like you would be interested in averting trouble, not stirring it up."

"Would you?" the major asked dryly.

"Yes, I would. I would think you'd be willing to share some of your cattle with the Indians who have none, who have no way of getting any, who aren't allowed to hunt."

"Then you are mistaken," the major answered. "I can't think of any justification for giving away army beef rations. What am I to do when my own men become hungry?"

"That's quite a way off, isn't it?"

"Not if I feed a thousand Apaches with our stores," the major pointed out with some accuracy. It wasn't the logic of the matter which aggravated Jessie; it was the coldness of the major's opinions. It was as if he wanted there to be trouble, as much trouble as possible. After all, there were promotions to be had, and a desk officer had never made rank as rapidly as a man in the field. The eyes of the major were hooded, expressionless—did he have other motives? Jessie had that thought suddenly descend upon her.

Laslo. Was it possible? They had made the analogy of military rank when discussing Laslo. Was he perhaps actually a military man? One in a position to stir up much trouble, to instigate bloodletting? A military commander in these far reaches had much power, after all. His commands were seldom questioned.

The dead Apaches on the ground weren't concerned with the answers to these questions. They had only been hungry; now they were dead.

"This will be reported to Washington," Jessie said. It was a meaningless threat and the major knew it.

"Fine," Neilsen replied. "Tell them that my men followed standing orders and turned away would-be poachers from army supplies by force of arms. I'll not persecute any of them for that. Or perhaps you think I shot these thieves myself?" Neilsen asked with a slight and challenging smile.

"We gain nothing here, Jessica," Ki said, seeing that Jessie was about to go well beyond losing her temper.

"No." She took a slow breath. "Nothing." She looked again at the dead Indians, knowing that the provocation aimed at the reservation Apaches was nearly irresistible, that they would now feel the need to strike back in some way, to break out, to attack, to announce physically and loudly their displeasure. "There will be trouble over this," she told the major, but he only smiled. He had all the guns, didn't he? What did it matter?

They rode away silently, Ki and Jessie. When they had traveled halfway to the reservation, they saw a rider coming from the south, a lean man riding a pale horse, but he was faceless in the shade of his hatbrim until he was nearly upon them and then they saw that it was Jake, Champ Corson's foreman.

He reined up in a cloud of dust, his face streaked with perspiration and dirt.

"Jake! What's wrong? What happened to Champ?"

"Nothing happened to Champ that I know of." The foreman wiped his forehead with the sleeve of his shirt and spat, settling his restless horse.

"I thought you'd gone to Mexico with him."

"Well, you was wrong," Jake said. He was, after all, a

77

charming man. "I was left to watch the home place. Champ didn't want to come back and find Firesky had burned it to the ground."

"Then what . . . ?"

"Give me a chance to talk, lady, and I'll tell you. Etting's found the herd."

"He's *what?*"

"Come in, saying he'd found the herd they took from the Sunset. I was ready to get the boys and ride, but he says to fetch you. I done it. You ready to ride?"

"I suppose." Jessie looked at Ki. Could they trust Jake enough to believe his story? The dark, narrow foreman wasn't one to encourage trust.

"There's not much else to do," Ki said. "The Indians need that beef, need it badly."

"What the hell's holding us up?" Jake demanded.

"Nothing. Nothing at all. Lead the way."

Jake eyed them darkly and then turned his horse, lifting it briefly into a run before he settled to an easy, dust raising trot. Ki and Jessie were left to lag behind the foreman.

"What's he up to?" Ki asked.

"We can't assume he's up to anything."

"No? Why did he come himself? It would have been more in character for Jake to send one of his hands to find us."

"I don't know what's in character for Jake."

"I know it, I know it. I don't like the feel of this. But if the ranger did succeed in finding that herd . . . how can we ignore the chance?"

"We can't, Ki. There'll be more killing, maybe a lot more if we can't come up with something for those reservation Apaches to eat."

They caught up with Jake and rode in silence toward the Sunset. The dust was thick; the desert empty, white; here

78

and there gray-blue sage broke the barren flats with dull color, and distantly there was a sinuous band of pale green to mark the course of the tiny stream which watered the Sunset grass.

The sun raked their backs, bored into their skulls. Jessica felt stunned by the heat, by the endless reaches over which they rode, desert which seemed to have no beginning and no end; although the chocolate-colored mountains, which seemed to border the depression, loomed larger with each mile, they seemed unreachable.

Jake had been looking back, at them they assumed, wondering why they had been lagging. Now his sour face drew itself into a bitter mask and as Ki and Jessie watched he reined in his roan roughly with one hand and with the other drew a blue-black Colt revolver from his worn holster.

Ki automatically reached for the bridle of Jessie's horse, reflexively began a movement which would have thrown himself and Jessica Starbuck to the earth, but it was obvious in the next fraction of a second that Jake wasn't drawing his gun to menace them.

"Who's that?" Jake demanded.

"Where?"

"There." The foreman, squinting into the sun, had seen a rider, dark and small, a mile or so behind. Even Ki who had glanced back occasionally had missed the approaching horseman.

"A soldier?"

"Soldiers don't ride alone," Jake said.

In another minute the three of them, sitting on their horses, side by side, were able to see just who the rider was.

"Nati."

"An Apache woman," Jake said.

"Wait."

79

"For what? We got some distance to cover."

"She may have important news for us."

Jake grumbled a disparagement and turned his horse, walking it slowly southward.

When Nati arrived she was winded, hot, her dark hair swirling around her head as she halted her spotted horse sharply, waving to Ki as she did.

"What is it, Nati?"

"Where are you going?" she wanted to know.

"Something has come up."

"Something has come up on the reservation! Three men were killed this morning trying to take army beef."

"We know that."

"Yes?" Nati seemed puzzled. Why, then, were they riding south, this woman who would be the Indian agent and her helper? "That is not all. They are councilling now. It is a council of war like in old times. They may try to break out. All of them at once."

"They can't. The army will shoot them down," Ki protested.

"They will try."

"The army has all the guns," Ki replied.

"Perhaps; perhaps not."

Ki looked at her, knowing that Nati knew something she would not tell even him.

"It's no good, Nati. Many will be killed. Women, old people, children."

"Perhaps," Nati replied. She held her head erect; her eyes looked straight ahead. "What else is there to do?"

"The Indian cattle," Jessie told her. "They have been found."

"Found?" Nati was skeptical. "Where?"

"We don't know. We're going to find out now," Jessie said.

"Is this something you are making up?" the Apache woman asked.

"No, Nati, it isn't. The herd has been found and it will be delivered to the reservation. Why don't you ride back and tell them that?" Jessie suggested.

"How can I?" She tossed her head. "How do I know it is true?"

"Don't you trust us, Nati?"

"Yes. Perhaps. And if I do?" she asked. "Do you know that the beef is coming for sure? Do you know when it will come? Can you make a promise that I can carry back to the reservation?"

Jessica answered truthfully, "No, Nati, we can't make a promise like that."

"I did not think so," she said sadly. "Besides, what good would the promise do? Would the council elders listen to me? Who am I but one who works with the white lady? My word means nothing. They wish to break out and so they will."

"They will die then."

"Yes, many will die. Many soldiers, many whites, many Apaches. And so what can we do?"

"Find those cattle," Ki said.

They caught up with Jake who looked at Nati with cast iron eyes, not bothering to ask who she was or what she was doing there.

"Where did you meet Dan Etting?" Jessica asked.

"Didn't meet him. A rider came in with a note."

"A rider?"

"That's right." Jake didn't look very happy about this. "A rider from the Wee-Hawk ranch south of us. Do I have to explain everything?"

"Just asking."

"You ask too much. Shut up and ride and you'll not have

81

to be asking all these questions."

They rode more tightly bunched now as they neared Sunset range. The ranch, even from a distance, seemed oddly silent, deserted. Champ Corson was gone into Mexico and with him two-thirds of his hands. Only Jake and a few of his most trusted people remained behind. It didn't feel good at all. Jessie kept trying to shake that feeling, but she couldn't—it just didn't feel good.

At the ranch they found the Wee-Hawk rider, the man who had supposedly brought the message from Etting to the Sunset. He was Mexican, wiry, dark, his hair silver although he appeared to be in his middle twenties. He had been in the bunkhouse with Jake's riders when the four of them arrived and someone was sent to bring him out.

He came, hat in hand, and stood, hip cocked to one side, hand resting on the butt of his revolver watching Jake and then Jessie whom he appreciated frankly.

"Mario, want to tell these folks what you told me?" Jake said.

Mario shrugged. "The man, the man Etting. He says come to sunset—have someone—get the lady and the tall man. Tell them he had find the cattle for the reservation."

"Where was this?" Jessie asked.

"Horn Creek," he answered. "At the pool."

"I'll show you," Jake said. He said it rather abruptly.

"And when was it?" Ki asked. Could they trust this Wee-Hawk man? He seemed honest, but there was too much at stake to risk all on first impressions.

"Yesterday in the afternoon. I saw the man as I watered my horse. He came to me and gave me this message."

"All right," Jake said. "Thanks, Mario. If you had something to eat, you best get riding toward the home range."

"Yes, I ate," the Mexican said.

Jake told Ki, "I'm getting my boys mounted up. You two wait here. Grab a bite at the big house if you want."

Then he swung down and Ki and Jessica were left alone. Alone but for Mario who had started toward his horse, a small pinto pony hitched to the rail beneath the cottonwoods. He stopped, hesitated, and returned.

"Señorita?"

"Yes?"

"I did not wish to say . . ." Mario looked toward the bunkhouse, "but this man Etting, he told me—'Make sure they come alone. Don't bring anyone else.'"

"Did he say why?"

"No, he said nothing else. Just that. I don't think he trusted this man Jake—perhaps I am wrong. Perhaps I dream as I walk, but I felt that. I only know that this is what he said: 'Tell the woman and the tall man that I've found the herd. For God's sake don't let Jake and his gang know.'"

"But he knows."

"I am sorry, Señorita. I have failed the man, but I did not know how to find you without Jake," he apologized.

"All right, it's . . ." then Jessie fell silent, for Jake had reappeared on the bunkhouse porch and with him were ten very hard, armed men. Mario glanced back once and then, putting his sombrero on his head, he bowed and walked quickly to his horse, riding swiftly off the Sunset Ranch.

Jake swaggered up to them. He put his hand on Jessie's horse's bridle and asked, "What was that about?"

"What?"

"The Mex? Did he have something to say to you?"

"Only good-bye—I think he was taken with me," Jessica said.

"Was he now?" Jake's eyes flickered darkly. "All right. Are you ready to ride?"

83

"Yes. Ready."

"Then let's do it, damn it. I want to find that beef and bring it home."

And Jessica Starbuck watched as Jake mounted and at the head of his men rode from the ranch; she couldn't shake the feeling, she just couldn't. Something evil was in the air. The man who led them into the hills—the man Etting hadn't wanted to know about this—seemed like nothing more than a bandit leader at the head of his small army.

There were too many people for Ki and herself to handle if it came down to it, too many if Jake proved to be Laslo ... and far too few if Firesky decided to make them his next war victims.

★

Chapter 8

The hills were dry, closing in around them as they rode higher into the land beyond the Sunset Ranch. The Horn, which was called a river on maps, was a quick-running, narrow freshet racing like a silver serpent through the yellow boulders along the canyon bottom. The sky was already orange; the deep shadows in the canyons were gathering into dark pools.

They rode silently. Jake was at the head of the small party, behind him a couple of the Sunset riders. Then came Jessica Starbuck and Ki with Nati a little way behind, lastly the remainder of the cowboys . . . if cowboys they were.

The trail rose into the jagged, rocky hills winding higher, following the deep gorge where the tiny river now ran.

They emerged on a narrow plateau where small clumps of grass spotted the gray, stony earth and a few wind-twisted cedar trees overhung the deep gorge below. Ahead Jessie could see the glimmer of late sunlight on a pool of water.

"That's where Mario met Etting if I'm not mistaken. The description matches. How many places like this can there be in the hills," Jessie said.

"Then where is Etting?" Ki inquired.

"Watching," Jessie said. "Waiting. He told Mario not to bring Jake up here, didn't he?"

"Yes, and now we have." Ki eyed the narrow, dark man who rode at the head of the party. At this hour the sunlight seemed to focus itself on the cartridge belts, the weapons carried by Jake and his men, causing them to glitter and dance, seemingly emphasizing their menace.

They were a hard crew recruited from the hardest of men in an area and a time when any man who rode this desert was hard. They had to be to survive. Champ Corson had surrounded himself with gunhands after being robbed blind by the cartel. The trouble was—and this thought had occurred to both Jessica and Ki—had Champ only surrounded himself with the very men who were robbing him? Was Jake really Laslo? These men cartel thugs?

They halted at the pool and the men swung down, loosening cinches, leading their horses to water.

"Well, where the hell is he?" they heard Jake ask. "The bastard said he was going to be here."

"There's been someone here," one of his riders, an Indian himself said, "I seen the sign of a single horse near the pool."

"Why don't he come in then?" Jake asked.

"Maybe he can't. Maybe the Apaches got him, or the rustlers," the Indian replied.

"Yeah, maybe," Jake said.

"Maybe," Jessie said, "Etting is just too smart for them. Maybe he knows who he's dealing with."

Ki nodded silently. Jake was walking toward them, swaggering, his leather chaps flapping with each step. He cupped his hands and lit the newly rolled cigarette between his lips.

"Well," Jake told them as he halted, picking a bit of tobacco off his lip, "I don't know where this fancy ranger is. And we can't go looking for him tonight. I reckon we'll have to make camp here—that is unless you two want to ride back."

"We can't very well negotiate that trail at night, can we?" Jessie pointed out.

Jake managed a thin smile. "No, I guess not." He turned and shouted out to his men, "Unsaddle. We're making camp here. Tom, get some lookouts organized. We're in Apache country."

There was no fire. Jessie and Ki sat on their bedrolls in the shadow of a great stone bluff seventy feet high, watching darkness settle over the desert, sharing a canteen of water, venison jerky and sourdough biscuits supplied by the Sunset ranch. On the rocks above them, lookouts with Winchesters perched. Jake himself had vanished. Neither Ki nor Jessie had seen him for a long while.

"Well?" Ki asked at length.

"Well . . . yes." Jessie shrugged. "I don't know, Ki. Things aren't going very well are they? Jake—is it him? Is it the major? The young lieutenant who seems to bungle everything but is always around? What good would it do us now to know *who* Laslo is? We couldn't feed the Apaches with the knowledge."

"Etting has supposedly found the herd."

"Supposedly. All of that is secondhand at best."

"Yes. If it was all true, where is he? Did Jake bring us up here on a pretext?"

"We have a lot of questions, Ki, don't we?" Briefly then she rested her head on Ki's shoulder as they sat watching the stars blink on.

Jessica asked, "Do you think Champ Corson is dead, murdered?"

"Why would you suggest that?" Ki asked. Jessie sat up, moving away from him.

"He's the last chance, isn't he? The last chance for beef provisions."

"Etting..."

"Yes, Etting. But where is he? Where is the ranger?" Jessica Starbuck asked, but Ki had no answer. The night which rushed in from the east had no answer. The stars hung bright and mocking in an ebony sky and Jessie moved away to roll up in her blankets and think, reaching no conclusion at all.

Ki could not sleep, did not even attempt it. He rose and walked along the plateau toward the pool which shimmered softly in the starlight and there Nati met him.

"You knew?" she asked, coming to him, gripping his shirtfront. "You knew I was waiting for you."

"Yes." He kissed her throat, feeling the pulse there, his hands encircling her waist, reaching for her firm curved buttocks, drawing her against him, feeling the insistent soft pressure of her pelvis. The excitement of the growing heft and rigidity of Ki's shaft against her stimulated desires which could only be satisfied in one way.

"Where?" she asked.

"Back there," Ki said. His blood was racing now; his ears ringing. He pulled Nati back for one last hard kiss, her parting lips pressing against his, brushing themselves against her teeth as her hand dropped to Ki's crotch, found him, stroked him through the fabric of his pants.

Together they staggered into the bushes beside the pool, Nati undressing as they went, pulling her blouse up overhead, revealing the strong slim line of her back, the smooth copper shoulders. She turned toward him, stepping from

88

her skirt, pressing her soft warm breasts against Ki, taking him down to the ground where he lay flat on his back as Nati unbuttoned his jeans tenderly, with great concentration, enormous pleasure, tugging them off as Ki fashioned a rough bed of her clothing and his.

She kissed his hard abdomen then, her dark hair trailing across his belly and his thighs as she enticed his rising need.

"You must not make me wait tonight," Nati said.

Ki had no intention of making her wait. He grabbed her by the shoulders and turned her. Nati straddled him in the night, crouching down across Ki's hips, her hands groping for his erection, finding it, centering it in her warm, damp softness, settling on him as Ki closed his eyes and let sensation overwhelm him.

Nati settled, his entire length sheltered within her. Her body twitched and her small inner muscles worked automatically against Ki's shaft, their stimulation bringing to his need an immediacy, and he began to arch his back, to drive into the Indian woman who was looking skyward now, to the stars and beyond, as Ki slid in and out, lifting her to a deep and explosive orgasm which shook her body.

Nati bent low, bracing herself on shaky arms, placing the nipple of her breast into Ki's mouth, pressing against his face as her hand groped behind her, finding his erection. Her finger slid down near the cleft of his ass, and she pressed against him until, with a sudden savage thrust, Ki filled her with his own rush of fulfillment.

Nati collapsed against him, kissing his chest, his lips; her hands rubbed his strong shoulders as the residual trembling of her body died away.

Shots rang out, a scream of pain followed, and they came to their feet suddenly. Ki grabbed for his jeans and was in them in seconds.

"What is it?" Nati wanted to know.

"Someone's attacking the camp."

"Who?"

"I don't know—run, Nati, run and hide."

"Come with me."

She grabbed his hand but Ki shook her off. "No, you go on. Jessica..."

"Come with me!" Nati again grabbed his arm. Toward the camp the sky was streaked with the crimson flashes of gunshots. The sound was a constant roar. They again heard the cry of pain from a man's throat.

"Go, Nati! Run!" Ki said again. What was happening to Jessica? Were the Apaches attacking the camp? Or the cartel... "Run!"

Suddenly it was too late to run. Three men burst through the brush, guns in hand, looking left and right. They might have passed if Ki and Nati had been silent, but Nati shrieked angrily and leaped for the nearest man who spun, started to shoot, and then merely clubbed her down.

Ki was among them suddenly, a whirlwind of elbows and knees, hands and feet, striking blow after blow against the bodies of the amazed men. He fought on, seeing one man go down and then another until the barrel of a Winchester repeater was slammed against his skull and he went down to lie twitching on the earth, Nati's screams and the cries of the wounded echoing in his ears, the battle roar following him down into a dark, spinning tunnel.

Jessica Starbuck leaped for her roll where her Colt revolver was concealed, but before she could find it in the dark, the wave of confusion broke over her.

The camp was alive with running, screaming men; bellows of anger, of pain, filled the air as the gunfire slashed at the darkness.

The pandemonium was complete. People shot without knowing who their targets were. A fire had started in the brush beyond the pool. Jessica saw the shadowy figures rushing at her from out of the darkness and she forgot the idea of finding her gun. She was going to get out of there, get out and find Ki.

A hand grabbed at her shoulder from behind and Jessica lifted her arm, smashing back with her elbow. The elbow found nose and a scream of pain rose from the throat of the man with the broken nose. Jessie ducked away and ran, his hand tearing a piece of cloth from the shoulder of her white blouse.

She had to leap over a dying man who clutched at her and go to the ground to hide in a pool of deep shadow as two men with torches rushed past her.

Not Apaches—they weren't Firesky's people. They were white, which meant they had to be cartel raiders, Jessie instantly decided.

Jake's men? No. Jake's men were fighting back. Champ Corson's people, heavily armed, well trained, were giving them hell, but it wasn't going to be enough—they were obviously outnumbered.

The fire was flaring up against the sky. Flames clawed against the night, rising to thirty feet and more as the spreading fire devoured the dry brush.

"Ki!"

She shouted but there was no answer. Who could have heard her above the roar and snap of the flames, the booming of the guns? Still she tried again, feeling a sinking feeling in her stomach.

"Ki!" But there was no answer from the night. She saw a raider rushing toward her and she snatched the derringer from behind her belt, firing at his legs, trying to take his feet from under him. One of the shots must have missed, but the raider was tagged, though higher than Jessie had wished. He cupped his groin with astonished hands, threw

91

back his head, and screamed in agony, falling on his face to the earth.

He had lost his rifle and Jessica started toward it, but before she could retrieve it, three other raiders spotted her and started toward her on the run. Jessie gave up the uneven battle and headed for the brush, into the cover of night, the thick mat of undergrowth that clotted the ravine below the narrow ledge.

A shot rang overhead, the bullet clipping brush beside her as she went to the ground, slithering forward, hearing the voices of her searchers behind her.

"Damn it, find the bitch."

"You find her if you can," a second voice shot back hotly.

"She's got a gun," a third voice added.

"A derringer!" the first man scoffed. "And it's empty."

"How the hell do you know she hasn't got more loads for it?"

"What damage can she do with that peashooter anyway, Frank?"

"Ask Adler—she shot his nuts off with it. I'm damned if I'm going into that brush after that Starbuck she-cat."

"Is that what you want me to tell Laslo?"

"Screw Las..." the voice broke off, astonished at its own temerity perhaps. "Where do you think she is?" the cartel thug asked with diffidence.

"I don't know. She can't be far—somewhere in the arroyo."

"We can seal it off; wait until daylight to find her."

"Better yet—set fire to the brush—look at that fire going across the clearing."

Jessie, too, lying with her cheek pressed to the earth not twenty feet from the searchers, could see the fire continuing to roar along the edge of the plateau. She shuddered at the thought of their setting fire to the arroyo where she hid.

"Oh, Ki, where are you?"

Perhaps he couldn't save her; perhaps he was already dead, but all of this would be easier to face with Ki, with imperturbable, sturdy Ki. But Ki wasn't there and he didn't hear her whispered words or the choked groan in her throat as the cartel men approached the arroyo with lighted torches.

Chapter 9

They touched fire to the brush and it leaped to flaming life. Jessica watched horrified, fascinated for a moment, seeing the silhouettes of the cartel men pasted against the fiery sky, and then, coming to her senses, she started away, crawling downslope through the sage, chia, manzanita, and sumac toward the arroyo bottom. The flame rushed after her, warming the night, filling the desert sky with the scent of destruction and death.

Jessie crawled and then began to run, rising up out of her crouch as the flames began to pop and snarl, to leap toward her as if they knew that she was there.

"There she goes!" someone yelled and a gun cracked.

"Damn you," their leader yelled. "Don't you know Laslo wants her alive. She's got a book with her."

In fact, she didn't have the black book with her, but that

might keep her alive for a time—until they searched her and decided they no longer had any reason to keep her alive. And Ki—what would keep Ki alive?

Jessie stumbled over a rock, pitched forward into a thick stand of sage, then rose and started on, face and hands scratched.

"Get her!"

The voice was astonishingly near at hand and Jessie turned to see a raider leap up out of the brush. She started to her right but the fire had caught a draft and was racing down the canyon there, forcing her back.

Then she was standing atop the bluff. It was thirty or forty feet to the bottom and she had no idea what was below. She could hear water running, but was the Horn more than a trickle at this point, or just a few inches of water useless for breaking her leap?—if she could jump, if she could bring herself to jump.

There wasn't much choice suddenly. The fire, running along the ridge like the wind hooked toward Jessica. She could feel the heat of her face, her hands, her breasts.

The dark men running toward her through the brush on the other side carried rifles and they shouted to her as they ran.

"Don't jump. Nothing's going to happen to you. You'll be safe."

They were cartel thugs. Jessie turned and jumped.

The thrill of it wormed up her spine as she fell an interminable fall into darkness. She heard other shouts, saw from the corner of her eye the fire along the shelf of the bluff above her. Below was only darkness, the narrow silver line of the Horn, the ground rushing up to meet her from out of the night.

When she hit, she hit hard.

The water was deep enough to break her fall, but not

deep enough to keep it from hurting. Jessica landed flat on her belly and her breath was knocked from her body. She could hear them shouting above her.

"She jumped."

"Get down there. Fast!"

"That fire..."

"Get down there! If we lose her, Laslo'll have a fit."

"Screw Laslo. That's a long way down. The fire's running down that arroyo. A man'd be lucky to get out of the canyon himself."

"Yes, and a man'd be lucky to live at all if he goes against Laslo. It's your choice."

Meanwhile Jessica had dragged herself, soaking wet and exhausted, into the brush beside the Horn. Smoke was wafting down the canyon, obscuring the stars, the men above her, the gun battle which continued to the north as Jake's people fought back the cartel thugs.

She could hear them now, sliding and slipping down the rugged slope, cursing, rattling guns and grunting with effort and pain. She crawled deeper into the brush, wondering still about Ki—was he alive or dead? And if he was alive, what in the world could she possibly do to help him?

Jessica got to her feet and in a crouch she began running through the heavy brush, hearing the pursuit behind her, the suddenly raised cry: "There she goes! After her! Damn all, don't let that woman get away."

She ran on frantically, the brush cutting at her arms and legs, her face. She leaped a narrow gorge, fell, knocked an elbow on a rock and started on, limping heavily. She fell again before she had reached the low, saw-toothed ridge stippled with nopal cactus. Looking back hurriedly she saw them coming on, six of them at least, closing in from either side of the dark canyon.

Jessica went on, her feet leaden, her lungs burning. She

was holding the painful twinge in her side when she crested the ridge at last and stood panting, looking back toward the crimson flames roaring down the opposite slope. The rest of the world was darkness, unfriendly and unpredictable.

She turned to start on and a man with a rifle loomed up suddenly before her.

"That's it, you bitch," he panted. "Stand still—I'm tired of running."

Jessie didn't hesitate. She knew enough *te* to handle most men, armed or not, and she side-kicked this one, trying to jar the rifle from his hands. It wasn't soon enough, quick enough. Her exhaustion slowed her down and the man, perhaps having been coached to expect something, jerked away from Jessie's kick.

Grabbing her arm, he threw her to the earth and stood over her, the muzzle of his rifle beneath a breast. There was nothing she could do then, nothing at all.

"Laslo wants to see you, little lady. Get up and let's get going."

There wasn't much choice but to comply. Slowly Jessica sat up, gathering her feet under her. Then as the rifleman backed away she got up, glaring at him from the darkness.

"Now! Let's go."

He waved the muzzle of his rifle, and at the same moment a dark shadow separated itself from the surrounding darkness and wrapped itself around him, taking him to the earth.

A silver knife flashed and Jessie heard the cartel man strangling on his own blood as he slumped to the earth and an Apache stood to face her, walking toward her with his hand still filled with the bloody knife.

Laslo walked across the scorched earth, moving with even strides, his polished boots menacing. Ki sat on the ground beside Nati, watching Laslo, the fire behind him and a ring of armed guards. The dead were scattered across the earth. Cartel men, Jake's men. Jake himself had survived although he had been wounded in the leg. He sat with a sneer on his lips, watching the tall cartel officer approach, halt spread-legged before them, and smile.

"Well, Ki, so it's over now, is it?"

"It's obviously over for the time being," Ki replied to Dan Etting, to Laslo. The boyish cartel officer who had the upper hand at the moment.

"Come now, you can't be so foolish as to expect to escape—to live to fight another day?" Etting laughed. His Texas accent had given way to one reminiscent of German.

"Perhaps," Ki said softly. He was bound hand and foot, but he thought that he could break his ankle bonds with a great effort. He knew he could slip the ties on his wrists— he had been born with the ability to disjoint the bones in his hands and practice had made him adept at it.

What then, however? Throw himself at Laslo and tear his throat out? What good would that do the Apaches on the reservation? What good would it do Jessica—and where was she? He assumed, hoped, prayed she had escaped and apparently she had.

"You will not fight again," Laslo said sternly, dogmatically. "I can assure you. You will be handed over to my superiors and once you have been questioned you will be negated."

"Negated—is that the term you use for murder?" Ki demanded.

"It cannot be called murder to remove the enemies of the cartel. We are the force of the future, the new world. You are a remnant of the old way."

"How'd you get to be an Arizona ranger?" Ki inquired.

99

"Did I say I was? That fool Champ Corson wrote for help. He wanted a ranger. I came and he accepted me as that. Fool."

"A fool? He only wanted to do what was right."

"And that will get him killed," Laslo snickered.

"He's dead?" Jake asked through the pain which had clamped his jaw shut. Laslo glanced his way.

"Not yet. He is bringing us more cattle from Mexico. Let him do that work for us, enrich us still more. Then let him die."

"She got away," Nati said out loud. All eyes shifted to her.

"What did you say, woman?"

"Jessica Starbuck got away," Nati repeated. "Otherwise we would be dead."

"Very perceptive for a savage," Laslo said. He hooked his thumbs into his gunbelt.

"She has gotten away?" Ki asked.

"For the time being," Laslo answered with a shrug. "There is no harm in admitting it. That's why you have been kept alive, Ki. You will be used to place pressure on Alex Starbuck's daughter. Let us see if she can stand to see her Japanese lover tortured."

"She is not my lover," Ki said forcefully but quietly.

"Oh, no, I have forgotten," Laslo said with mock sincerity. "You are an honorable man. And, of course, you prefer savages like this thing." He touched Nati with his boot toe and Ki nearly gave in to the provocation, nearly leaped to attack the Prussian. "If you hadn't been secreted in the bushes with her, you might have done something to help your patroness, isn't that so? How can you consider yourself noble—lying with a savage? How can any of you consider yourselves noble? You do not know what nobility is, what right action is. You are slaves of democracy."

Jake said through his pain, "And what the hell are you, you struttin' little bastard? You got no loyalty—not like the Chinee's got for that woman, like I got for the brand, like the Indian girl here's got for her people on the reservation. What do you live for, you posturin' little bastard?" Jake spat and Laslo kicked him in the face, snapping his head back. Jake went over, out cold, blood trickling from his nostrils, from his ears.

Laslo said, "His conversation wasn't interesting."

Ki swallowed a sharp retort. There wasn't anything to be accomplished by antagonizing the icy cartel man. "What do we do now?" he asked.

"We wait. We wait until the Starbuck girl is found," Laslo replied.

"And then?"

"And then there will be nothing else to wait for," the Prussian said and there was nothing in the least amusing in the way he said it. Laslo turned away then, hands folded behind his back and, with the fire silhouetting him, he walked from them, leaving his guards to watch Ki and Nati.

"There isn't long," Nati said. Her hair was loose around her shoulders.

"There is much time." Ki looked at her and smiled.

"No. Who will come? Who can save us? Who would bother? The army perhaps?" She laughed at that notion, shaking her head.

"We will survive."

"I don't think so. And so I want to say, Ki—I am happy to have known you, very happy."

Ki smiled, "And I am happy to have known you, Nati."

"Even with Skull?"

"Even with Skull and his temper. He only did what he did because he cared for you. I can understand that."

"Can you?" she asked.

"Of course. Who would not care for you, Nati?"

"Ki—they will kill us, won't they?"

He hesitated and then decided not to lie. "Yes," he answered, "they will kill us. Now or later. They can't leave us alive, can they?"

"No." She paused. "It is all right, Ki. All right. I have known you."

Ki nodded in silence. What kind of answer could he make to a statement like that? It was all right with her if she died because of Ki. Well, it wasn't all right with Ki himself. She would not die, nor would Jessica—wherever she was. He did not know how he would fight back, how he could overcome the impossible odds, but he swore an oath there and then that he would fight back, that he was far from being finished.

"Are you all right?"

Jessica rubbed her forehead. She looked across the tiny fire at the man with the long dark hair, the man who wore a white shirt, a red sash, and a red headband. The man called Firesky.

"I'm all right."

"Good." The Apache poked at the fire with a stick. "You suddenly collapsed. There is a knot on your head. You must have fallen somewhere."

"I did," Jessica replied. She touched the knot just behind her ear. She now recalled striking a rock as she leaped to the Horn. The Apache was watching her closely and Jessie met his gaze.

"Lucky for me you were around."

"Yes."

"Now what do you intend to do with me?" she asked directly.

He shrugged. "You are the Indian agent?"

102

"Yes. Temporarily. I'm really looking to find out what's been happening to the Indians' supplies."

"Stolen."

"Yes, I know that. I mean I wanted to know who is taking them and how and where they are being kept."

"What makes this your business?" Firesky wanted to know.

"The people who I think are responsible for everything are enemies of mine, old enemies."

"Yes?" Firesky lifted an eyebrow. "The soldiers?" he asked.

"No, not the soldiers. They're not responsible for the thefts."

"I think they are."

"No."

"This Major Neilsen, I know him. He is the sort to do that, to make a war."

Jessica nodded thoughtfully. "He's the type, but he's not responsible."

"It doesn't matter who. They are white."

"Maybe it *does* matter. Look at Corson—do you know him? He's mortgaged his ranch to try to buy a herd of beef in Mexico to deliver to your people on the reservation."

"Mortgaged?"

Jessie explained that as best she could. Firesky shook his head in disbelief. "Why would he do that?"

"He feels a sense of obligation."

"He is white," Firesky replied.

"Don't judge him so quickly. You don't like all Apaches to be lumped together, do you?"

"All Apaches are honorable," Firesky said stiffly.

"All right. They are if you say so. Why are you here, Firesky? Why did you come to my aid?"

It was a moment before he answered. The fire was burning low. It glowed crimson, black, and deep gold as Firesky poked at it again. He lifted his eyes to hers finally.

"I am here because strangers were here. On my land, on my desert, near my people."

"Yes?" she prompted patiently.

"And I helped you because . . . because since I saw you that night—you know that night?—I have longed for you, thought of you, dreamed of you. I have imagined you lying beneath me, lying as you were that night, naked and pale and ready to accept me . . . I am sorry."

"Sorry? There's nothing wrong with it. What do you think I have been thinking of since you crept in my window, Firesky? Since I saw you over me with a knife in your hand, with your eyes gleaming, with your body tensed and eager."

"You cannot mean it?"

Jessie laughed. So he was shy beneath it all, this wild Apache prince, this feared warrior, this man with the broad shoulders and smoldering eyes, with the animal attraction Jessie could feel with each small movement he made. Those movements dried her mouth and started tiny warm streams trickling inside her.

"You cannot mean it," he said again and he moved toward her, hovering over her as she bent her face up to his and her hand crept up his thigh, drawing him nearer yet.

"But I do mean it, Firesky," Jessica Starbuck said and she lay back, drawing the Apache war leader down to her.

★

Chapter 10

His name was Firesky and people said that he was a butcher, a bloodthirsty warrior, an outlaw, and a scourge. He was also a man, exciting, strong, compelling. Jessica Starbuck lay beside the fire, wriggling out of her skirt, opening the buttons of her blouse to reveal her full, pink-nippled breasts to the hungry eyes of the Apache.

She stretched out her fingers and wriggled them impatiently, calling him to her, and Firesky slipped from his own trousers and shirt to go down beside her in the warm night.

Jessie reached out and found his warm, pulsing erection. Her hand encircled it, slowly stroked it, her thumb working across the sensitive head of his shaft as Firesky lowered his lips to her breasts, abdomen, thighs, kissing her everywhere at once as she gently manipulated him, stroked him, and reached behind him to let her finger trace the line of his back.

He looked into her eyes and found her smiling, found the warmth of her invitation real and irresistible. Jessica met his lips with a lingering kiss, her tongue darting into his mouth, her arms wrapped tightly around his shoulders.

Then without speaking she rolled to hands and knees, waiting for Firesky to ease up behind her, waiting for his erection to touch her soft inner flesh. She reached back, moaned softly, her fingers intertwining with his as they guided his hardness into her moist inner recess. She shuddered and lifted her head to gasp with delight and Firesky pitched forward to lean against her, bracing himself with one hand, letting his other find her breasts, toy with and tease her taut nipples as he sank into her to the hilt. Jessica again softly moaned.

Firesky was bucking against her now almost uncontrollably as he plunged into her warmth, and Jessie collapsed face downward against the earth, Firesky mauling her, opening her to accept his passion completely, deeply.

He groped for her crotch, finding where he entered her, parting her with his fingers, touching her.

Jessie was filled with his warmth, with the drive and need of the man, with the excitement of his body, and she spread her legs as far as they would go, inviting him still farther, feeling him drive against her. She felt his probing, greedy fingers, his lips and teeth across her back and buttocks, up the back of her neck where her blonde hair lay in a soft tangle. She sensed the growing urgency of the man until with a sudden hot rush he filled her, and Jessica's own body released an answering gush, leaving her body drained and trembling.

Jessica rolled over without losing him. She wrapped her arms around his neck, drawing him down to her. She kissed him almost with violence as he lay panting against her, shaking in the night as if it were cold and there were no warm fire beside them.

It was pleasant, comfortable, her body adjusting to him,

the lingering sensation warm and delightful, and Jessica could have stayed like that for a long, long while if it weren't for one thing.

"Ki," she said.

"Ki?"

"The man who travels with me. He is a prisoner back there. He and the Apache woman, Nati."

"Nati. Yes, I know her." Firesky had been smiling but now he frowned. She could feel him slipping away from her. It was with regret that she let him go, but there was far too much to be done.

She dressed, speaking to Firesky all the while. "Laslo, as he calls himself, works for a large cartel, a group of men who are stealing all the beef, most of the supplies from the reservations. It doesn't sound like much, does it? Think what it costs to feed half a million people a year! And so the Apaches on the Bowie reservation are hungry."

"They won't be—for long."

"What do you mean?" She touched his bronze shoulder and he shrugged.

"You know what I mean."

"You're talking about leading them off of the reservation."

"Yes," the Chiricahua said, "that is what I mean."

"You can't."

"Of course, I can. They are hungry."

"Then we'll find a way to feed them."

"And they are slaves," Firesky said angrily.

"They are at least safe on the reservation. You can't be thinking of taking old women and children into the hills to fight again. What can become of them?—you should know by now Firesky."

"You want me to surrender, to give up my own freedom, my manhood!"

107

"I wouldn't tell you to do anything of the sort," Jessica replied. "But how can you think that you're doing others a favor by bringing them out on the desert again? With Major Neilsen around? Nothing would make him happier than to have a mass breakout."

"So that he can kill more Apaches!"

"Yes! Just that. And if you let it happen, then you're partly responsible, aren't you?"

The Apache was quiet for a long while. He shook his head heavily. "The war must go on."

"Why?" Jessie said, clenching her hands, looking pleadingly at the warrior.

"Because it is right!" He stood and turned his back to her. "Because this is our land!"

"Because you fought for it, died for it?"

"Yes!" He spun back.

"And so if the Americans fight for it, die for it, then it is theirs?"

"You do not understand me—there is nowhere left for the Apache to go. We are hunted in Mexico, hunted in the United States."

"Then perhaps the time has come to live in peace, to recognize that a new day has come."

"Never," Firesky said very quietly, and she knew that on that point he was unshakable. He would never surrender, not until he was buried on the desert.

"But the others, Firesky—they cannot fight. And they will die."

"Perhaps. They will die free," he said, sounding a little uncertain.

"The children."

"Yes!"

"And the old who cannot hobble away? Those who wanted only peace?"

"Because they cared more for their bellies than for their souls!" Firesky said bitterly.

Jessica walked to him and put her hand on his shoulder. "Firesky, it was their choice. They care for their bellies because they don't wish to see the old starve, their children crying, hungry. It's not wrong."

"It is soft."

"All right. It's soft. It's their choice, nonetheless," Jessica said.

"I think they will fight. I think in time they will join me again."

"Hungry or fed?"

"Either way!" he answered sharply.

"Then let's do our best to feed them. In the meantime, let's fill their bellies. That can't be wrong, Firesky, can it?"

"Jessica . . . what does that name mean in English? 'hard-headed woman'?" Firesky asked, but he was smiling, turning to her, taking her into his arms. "All right. I will try to help you. Try to help you free your friend and Nati and feed the reservation Indians. It will only make things harder for me, you know? They will have to grow dissatisfied again, grow hungry again before they will join me—more than a few young adventurous boys."

"And you, you are making it easier for all of your people."

"Let us hope so," Firesky said softly.

"Do you have your warriors near here?" Jessica asked. "Enough so that we can get Ki out of Laslo's hands?"

"I have no one nearby, Jessica," Firesky said and Jessie could only stare at him.

"No one?"

"My men are in the south, raiding. I stayed behind vowing to kill the crooked Indian agent. Then I stayed longer because of a woman."

"But that can't . . . how are we going to do what has to be done, the two of us?"

"You will tell me, Jessica. I am sure that you will have an idea what must be done." Then he laughed and kissed her and Jessica Starbuck laughed in response, but it didn't take long for the smile to fade. Firesky might be sure she had an idea, but she hadn't even a glimmer of one. She looked back across the canyon where still the dying fire glowed, where Laslo held Ki and Nati prisoner. Perhaps there *was* no way. An idea, heavy, dark, came to her suddenly and she had to push it away mentally. Of course, there was a way—hadn't she and Ki always come up with something, even when things looked hopeless?

But Ki was over there and she was standing here beside Firesky feeling small and for once rather helpless until with a shrug, a deep fortifying breath, she turned back to the Chiricahua and said, "There's a way and we'll find it."

Firesky laughed again. He picked up his weapons from the ground. He carried a bow and arrows, a Henry repeating rifle which he now gave to Jessica, not bothering to ask her if she could use it—of course, she could, this competent and amazing white woman.

Then he asked, "Now?"

"Now," she answered resolutely, and they started off toward Laslo's camp, having no idea what they would do to free Ki and Nati, only knowing that they would try, and failing, they would join them in their imprisonment. And death, for there wasn't much doubt what Laslo would do with them after there was no longer a reason to keep them alive, after he had tortured Jessie for the information he needed. That would be what they had instructed him to do, she was positive. Find out what she knew for sure, where the records were, who else knew anything about the cartel— they could be eliminated later.

The cartel had known Alex Starbuck, powerful, righteous, determined, and they knew his daughter. They knew that she would never quit until she was dead.

And so they would oblige.

With Firesky she worked her way over the burned ridge toward Laslo's camp. She assumed he had appropriated the campsite Jake and his men had made the previous night. The scent of dead fire was heavy in the air. The ground underfoot was hot. Now and then as their feet turned over ash, red footprints glowed against the dark earth. There was a pale, waning moon rising and behind the lingering smoke, stars throbbed silently. There was no fire in Laslo's camp— perhaps they had seen enough fire—but they could see men moving around and hear the pitiable moans of a man, perhaps the man who had had his testicles shot off by an insignificant derringer.

Jessica still had no idea how to handle this. They were so outnumbered as to make the idea of rescue laughable. Still they couldn't leave Ki there. Something had to be done.

The idea was so obvious she wondered why it had taken so long for it to occur to her. She told Firesky as they lay on the bluff above the camp, looking down.

"There is a risk," the Apache said, "a risk to your friend and to Nati."

"I didn't expect to find a way without a risk," Jessie answered.

"No." The Chiricahua looked down into the canyon. It was like peering into a deep, dark well. They could see little. There was only the moaning. What was in his thoughts,

111

she wondered. It was a battle he planned now, as he had planned many battles. Was he weighing this consequence and that, or only thinking of the hungry on the reservation, knowing that these men were a part of those who had taken their food?

"Well, Firesky?"

"I have no better solution," he admitted.

"Well, then, how do you want to handle it?"

"I'll go down. Give me fifteen minutes," the Apache war leader said. "Then you can start."

"Firesky" she said as he turned away. When he looked back he was met by a kiss, soft, damp, warm.

"You're a hell of a man...in a lot of ways," Jessica Starbuck told him.

Then he was gone, working his way downslope through the thick brush as silent as the night breeze which shifted Jessie's hair, drifting an unnoticed strand across her face.

She stood and watched and waited, glancing at the moon and hoping that it didn't shine too brightly that night and reveal her plot. There was too much at stake—a chance to strike a telling blow at the cartel, Ki's life.... She decided not to dwell on how important it all was but to wait patiently, as stoic as the moon, to prepare her forces for the battle to come.

Firesky worked his way down the hill. The brush was like dark water rising all around him. He could smell the camp now, see the men standing watch. Clumsy, they were very clumsy. No matter—they could kill and so he had to be careful with the worst of them.

He was within fifty feet of the clearing verge now, so he went to his belly, slithering silently forward, his searching hands finding dry twigs which might give his presence away, moving them aside as he crawled forward to where he could see directly into the camp.

He could see the leader of the whites, this Laslo, standing with two of his men, a rifle in his hands. Across the clearing Nati and Ki sat back to back. The girl was asleep, Firesky thought, but the man seemed to be only pretending to sleep. He would be ready when he had to move; that one would always be ready.

And now Firesky, notching an arrow, laying the rest of his arrows out before him in easy reach, was himself ready. He looked to the bluff where the woman waited, counting the minutes, and he settled in, anticipating the fight that was to come, the fight which would take many lives— perhaps the wrong ones. Perhaps his own.

A warrior doesn't concern himself with such things. He fights and when he has fought well he accepts that which comes—victory or defeat, life or death.

Someone in the camp cried out and Firesky rose to one knee, drawing back his arrow, letting it fly.

★

Chapter 11

Ki's eyes flickered open. He saw the pointing arms, saw the sleeping men roused. On the bluff the fire had come to life again and now it curled and snapped down the canyon toward them, threatening the camp itself.

"Damn you! It was stupid to start that fire," Laslo shouted.

"We had to get the girl, Laslo."

"Yes, and where is she? Get everyone up, get saddled. The wind's driving it right down our throats. Move it!"

The arrow passed so near that Ki heard it whip past. He himself was an archer, a deadly archer. He had studied *kyuba no michi,* or the way of the bow and horse, and his masters had declared him competent. He knew the twenty-four arrows, the *nakazashi,* knew their uses, and was expert with each. But he knew that the hand and the eye behind the bow that he now saw put to use were naturally skilled, adept from birth, trained from childhood with their use. He knew it was an Indian warrior who used the deadly tools now.

At first he thought there had to be more than one attacking Apache, for no sooner had the first arrow imbedded itself with a soft *thunk* into the chest of a cartel thug than a second arrow buried itself in the abdomen of the man next to Laslo. A third pierced the throat of yet another badman who staggered across the camp, gurgling on his own blood, trying to break off the shaft.

Yet all of the arrows had been fired from the same position, and so it had to be one man—one who could notch an arrow, draw the bow, and fire with deadly accuracy every few seconds.

Without consciously considering it, Ki knew this man was not an enemy. He and Nati were nearest the archer, yet they alone appeared not to be targets.

"What is it?" Nati's voice was taut with excitement but not broken by fear. She was, after all, Apache. As she opened her eyes, brought awake by Ki's sudden tensing, by the cries of the wounded and dying, she saw the fire roaring toward the camp.

Ki didn't answer immediately, but in less than ten seconds he had slipped his hands free of their bonds and was now untying his ankles. Nati could only stare at the flames, at the men with arrows in them. Now the cartel men began to fire back blindly, having no clear targets, but needing to answer death with their own noise and thunder.

Ki was untying Nati's wrists as Laslo rushed up, grabbing at his shoulder. Ki ducked and hip-rolled him, throwing him to the earth beyond, his rifle clattering free.

Laslo had continued his roll and come to his feet with surprising quickness. He wasn't a *te* adept, but he was

116

young, strong, and eager. He launched himself at Ki who didn't turn in time to keep from being slammed to the earth, where he and Laslo grappled as Nati finished untying her ankles and rose unsteadily.

A cartel man grabbed her by the arm. Nati, furious, tried to knee him in the groin, but he turned away and her knee glanced harmlessly off his thigh. An arrow from the brush ended the brief struggle.

As Nati watched, the arrow thudded into his back and with his eyes rolling back, his hand pawing futilely at the shaft of the arrow, he toppled forward onto his face.

"Run for it!" someone shouted.

The fire was nearly to the camp, sweeping faster than anyone could have anticipated down the gorge, roaring and crackling, leaping against the sky. Nati saw the pale moon behind the smoke as she turned and tried to help Ki.

She wasn't much help. Laslo saw her from the corner of his eye and slapped her back with his forearm. Ki, whirling, kicking, delivered one glancing *choku-zuki* blow and another which landed solidly beneath Laslo's heart. Ki took a surprisingly good right hand hook from the tall redheaded man in response. Ki smiled. There was no joy in it if there was no contest in the battle.

The second hook missed Ki's temple but Laslo who was not about to give up, kicked out and landed solidly on Ki's kneecap causing him to back up a step, sidekick in retaliation, and follow Laslo toward the edge of the outcropping, to where Jessica had made her leap into the Horn hours earlier.

Laslo was beaten now. Ki could see it on his face, see that he knew it as he futilely tried to block Ki's crisp, masterly blows which cut at him like razors, striking hip and shoulder, abdomen and heart.

117

"Now? Now will you give it up?" Ki asked. "Tell us where the cattle have been taken."

"Yes!" Laslo cried out loudly. Behind Ki the fire still raged. Jessica had learned well, learned to turn their terrible weapon back on them, for there was no doubt at all in Ki's mind that it was Jessie who had started the fire above the cartel camp.

"I give up. I surrender," Laslo said and he hung his arms, his head.

"You will tell us what you know?"

"Yes," he panted, touching his forehead which was bloody, breathing in deeply as he held up his other hand, fending Ki off. "Whatever you want to know."

"Speak then, and quickly."

"Just a minute . . . can't breathe."

Ki waited then, crouching slightly, not entirely trusting this cartel officer. They could learn much of the cartel's workings from Laslo if he spoke openly, perhaps enough to be able to anticipate their next move and cut them off before they could begin, certainly enough to finish the cartel's reservation chicanery, and with luck much more. Did Laslo know, for example, the identities of the men at the head of the pyramid, those who had actually ordered the death of Alex Starbuck and his wife?

For now, however, Ki was impatient to learn one simple fact—the location of the stolen cattle herds.

"Speak, Laslo."

"Damn you to hell, Ki! Damn you and that Starbuck bitch eternally. This is the end of my career!"

Then Laslo turned, and with Ki diving at his heels, feeling a boot slip through his fingers, the cartel officer ran for the edge of the bluff and leaped into space, falling toward the shallow creek below. A crazed laugh mingled with fear

118

filled the night. Ki rose and went to the edge of the bluff to stand staring down. He could see nothing but the ribbon of a stream.

"Ki!" Nati grabbed his arm and turned him. "The fire, Ki, it is nearly upon us."

It was at that. A wall of flame thirty feet high and rising, reaching out as if to grab them with crimson and gold talons. All of the fighting had stopped as men ran for safety, not all of them finding it as the fire storm swept down the canyon.

"Which way?" Nati said, gripping Ki's right hand with both of her own, her fingers kneading his flesh, her eyes bright. "Over the edge? Into the river?"

"No." Ki didn't think Laslo had survived the fall and he didn't think that he and Nati would have a much better chance of making it. "This way."

He took her by the arm and guided her along the edge of the bluff. He had seen, had thought he had seen a declivity farther south. Now by the hot glare of the fire he could see nothing at all. Smoke swirled around his feet. Nati was choking, staggering blindly after him.

"Dear Jessica," Ki said to himself. How ironic it would be if they were killed by the flames Jessie had started to set them free. Unfortunately, Ki himself wouldn't be around to appreciate the irony.

"There!" Ki said. Before them a deep, dark cleft opened in the ground and Ki dived for it, taking Nati with him. The fire, creating its own heated wind, now swept over them as Ki ripped off his vest and covered Nati's head with it. He held his breath and closed his eyes, pressing her to the ground as the flames leaped the narrow, brushless arroyo and continued leaving the acrid, fearful scent of fire behind.

A long while later the smoke cleared. Ki lifted his head

and blinked, the heat still washing over him, although the flames had passed on to work their way down toward the Horn, leaving the ravaged, scarred land blackened and barren.

"It is gone?" Nati asked, peering from beneath Ki's leather vest.

"It is gone." He smiled, kissed her, and helped her to her feet, recovering his vest with its supply of *shuriken* in its many pockets. "Come." He climbed up and pulled Nati after him and together they started walking across the scorched land toward the camp, Nati moving gingerly as the embers scorched her moccasins. Ki seemed impervious to the heat as he seemed impervious to so many things, not above them, but merely distant from them in a way Nati didn't entirely understand.

It didn't matter. He was there. Strong and sure and handsome. He was a good man, a good friend, a gentle and deft lover. She gripped his hand tightly once, smiling up at Ki before she let go and walked on, arms folded beneath her breasts.

As they approached the camp, Ki began to circle and move more slowly, glancing back frequently at Nati, gesturing to her. There had been twenty or more cartel men in that camp—a single Apache warrior with bow and arrows hadn't killed all of them.

Who was the Indian who had come to their aid? Ki knew it had to be an Indian, and in this area an Apache, but unless Jessica had friends he hadn't met, he couldn't imagine who— certainly not Skull. Although he would have tried to save Nati, his first arrow would have been aimed at Ki.

"Hey, Chinee!"

Ki stiffened and stopped, hands on hips, looking toward the burned over camp. Jake stood there, his dark narrow

120

face twisted, his shirt ripped, trousers out at the knee. He had a rifle in his hand.

"China boy, can't you hear me?"

Ki looked skyward, praying for patience. Jake had struck him wrong since the day they met and things hadn't improved much. Still he seemed to be on the right side, seemed to be one of the few allies Ki and Jessie were likely to find on the desert.

"I hear you," Ki said, grumbling another few words under his breath. Then with Nati he walked to the camp. Four more of Jake's riders emerged from the shadows to stand in the smoky moonlight beside the Sunset foreman. All of them were armed—the cartel had lost some men in the battle following the fire, after all.

"Where you been, Chinee?"

"Look, Jake..."

"That fire scattered everyone. Charlie here and Lou had already cut themselves loose with a knife. Lou carries a boot knife and these damned rustlers didn't find it. Say," Jake rubbed a knuckle vigorously against his forehead where a huge knot had sprouted, "did you know some of these people who raided us can't even speak English—nor Spanish. What kind of foreigners were they?"

"It's not important, Jake, what is important..."

"What's important now," Jake interrupted again, "is to find that herd they got hidden up in the hills."

"If we can, yes."

"Hell, yes, we can. Only reason we didn't find it before is because the wrong man was looking. We had this Etting out searching, and he would come in and say, 'Oh, I can't find hide nor hair of them cattle.' Course not, the bastard was one of 'em, wasn't he?"

"Yes, he was."

121

"And what kind of foreigner was he?" Jake demanded. "I heard him talking some lingo I never heard. Deutsch, maybe—once had me some Deutscher neighbors in Pennsylvania, good folks, before I drifted."

Jake had suddenly become garrulous, perhaps the excitement of the evening had stimulated him to this excess of talkativeness. Ki didn't really want to hear Jake's life story, and so he cut him off.

"All I know is that they tried to kill us, and if we don't find some cattle and take them to the reservation, a lot of other people *will* be killed. Also, Champ Corson will be broke."

"He'll lose his shirt anyway," the man named Charlie said. He was short and thick as a barrel.

"No, he won't. If we can recover the stolen beef, Champ can sell the Mexican herd himself—and make enough to pay you men the fighting wages you deserve."

"He's right," Jake said. "Come daylight, we start looking ourselves."

"The rustlers," Ki said, "still won't be willing to give up those cattle, and by my guess they outnumber us three to one."

Jake disagreed, "I know rustlers, Chinaman, hear me? They find out we're on their trail and they'll damn sure run. Their boss is dead and the border's close. Bet on it. They'll be gone."

"Maybe. Jake, these people aren't your regular cattle rustlers. They're part of an organized army. They can't run to Mexico and get away from their bosses. They wouldn't think of it, anyway. They'll fight to the last man, I think."

"Foreigners," Jake said, scratching his chin.

"That's right."

"An army, you say—you mean that?"

"I'm afraid so. There may be a hell of a lot more of them somewhere. Remember the first herd? It had to have been driven to the coast, or so Champ told me. Where are the men who did that? On their way back, I expect," Ki told the foreman.

"What the hell are these people up to, Chinaman? I can't see it. I fight for the brand that pays me—for Sunset and Corson, but I don't get this other business about them being some sort of army, all of them some kind of foreigners."

"You don't get it? These are people who want the Indians to starve to make trouble. They are against Corson, against this country. They are an army, and I call them that with reason—this is a war, Jake."

"A war against America?" Charlie asked dubiously.

"Yes. In a way."

"Don't make sense."

"Yes," Ki said, "it does. They don't have to fight us head-on. They sneak and steal and undermine, bribe corrupt politicians and merchants, cut links of communication, poison and steal, incite internal dissension. Why, if they can use the Apaches to kill the Americans and vice versa, they're damn well pleased with themselves."

"And they pick up the leavings."

"That's it," Ki said. "They pick up the leavings."

"Smart."

"They are smart, and they're dirty. They're waging a war which is invisible to most of the country. You men have seen it; you've seen your friends go down, battle casualties in this war. I'm telling you this so that you won't think it's going to be easy, so that you'll know that it's important."

"Hell, Chinee, we knew that. They got us down and they think they got us beat. They don't. We're with you all the way."

123

"Good. Jake, you must have a fair idea of where those cattle can be."

"Sure. Roaring Slope. I would have gone there right off and found them steers, but Etting said he had already been there. The only place for a long way you'll find plentiful water and graze both."

"Where is that?"

"Up high." Jake lifted his chin. "Top of the saw-toothed ridge. It's a deep canyon. There's plenty of cedar trees, some pine up there. Called Roaring Slope because of the wind that's always blowing through there. It's very high up so it's cool most of the time. Plenty often it'll rain up there and never reach the flats."

"Fine. That's where we'll look first. How many men have we got altogether?"

"Those you see here, three more standing watch now. What's that make, Charlie?"

"Ed died."

"Eight, I guess," Jake said.

Ki frowned, it wasn't enough. "That'll have to do, I guess."

"Yup, it will. Don't worry—these boys are tough."

Ki hoped so. It still looked like an uphill fight to him. Charlie asked, "Them arrows? Someone was out there killing the rustlers when we broke through. Someone started that fire up again. They thought the wind had shifted and fanned it, but you can't kid me. It was set. And just who in hell did that?"

"It was..." Ki began, but he was cut short by a voice from the shadows. They all turned that way, nervous thumbs drawing back the hammers on the rifles they held.

"I started the fire," Jessica Starbuck said, looking weary,

124

smudged, exquisite. "As for the arrow—well, those came from the bow of my friend here." And the rifles that had been cocked were lifted and sighted as the Apache renegade, Firesky, came into the clearing.

★

Chapter 12

"It's Firesky," Jake said, "kill the son of a bitch!"

They would have done it, too, but Jessica Starbuck stepped right in front of the Apache warlord and there wasn't a man there who was going to take a chance on shooting a woman like that. After all you could spend the rest of your life on that desert and never hope to see another female put together like that one.

Firesky was behind Jessie, tense and ready, his dark eyes flashing.

"Ki—you're all right. I was afraid I'd roasted you. The way that fire came down the slope . . . it was more than I'd expected."

"I'm all right," he said. "And you—I didn't know what had happened to you."

"I'm all right, thanks to Firesky." She raised her voice, "All of you are alive thanks to Firesky."

"Fine, now step aside, lady, and let us shoot down the son of a bitch."

"Don't you understand! He saved your lives."

"Don't you understand, Miss Starbuck? This man's responsible for the deaths of scores of people across this territory—some of 'em friends and relatives. The war don't end just because you say so."

"I'm not trying to end the war," Jessie said, leaning forward at the waist, speaking emphatically. "I'm trying to prevent the next one. We've all got one aim in common— finding that cattle herd and getting it to the reservation. That's all."

"With Firesky behind us."

"He's not going to attack you by himself."

"He doesn't have to, does he? The hills are loaded with Apaches."

"He's here under a truce, Jake. Don't you understand that? He's helped free you and now he wants to help find the cattle."

"To take them for himself," Jake replied.

"To deliver them to the reservation as I told you," Jessica said in exasperation.

Ki stepped in, "Jake, if the man has given his word..."

"And what the hell good's an Apache's word!"

"He didn't come here because he wanted to make war— that would be a little insane, walking in here, wouldn't it?" Ki asked.

"I don't know what he's got in his mind. He's got nerve, sure, but I never heard anyone say he was a peaceloving man."

Firesky put his hand on Jessie's shoulder and stepped around her as the rifles came up again. He walked toward Jake, bow and arrows still in hand. He halted six feet away

128

from the Sunset foreman and stared at him with cool contempt for a long minute.

"If I had wanted to kill you, I would have. You know that. I am here because the woman has convinced me that it is best for the reservation people. For myself, I don't care about the beef. If you do, let us work together. When this is over, then we can begin our war again. You may kill me—or," he shrugged, "I may kill you, Jake."

"It'll have to be one way or the other next time we meet," the foreman said. Then, shaking his head he added, "I must be crazy, but I'll take his word for it—his word that he'll not draw his bow on us until this is done. Charlie?"

Charlie lifted his shoulders and spat. "I'm crazy too, I guess. I'll go along with it."

"Then that's . . ." Jessie began. Jake interrupted her sharply.

"But if this is a trick, Firesky, if this is a plan to get those beef and have our scalps at once, then so help me I'll kill you if I have to claw my way back out of the grave to do it."

"And if you betray me, Jake, you will not have to wait so long for my vengeance. My people will come. They will know you; you will die."

It wasn't exactly an auspicious beginning to the alliance, but for the time being the uneasy truce would have to do. Ki made a practical suggestion. "We don't know where the cartel men have gone or how many of them there are. They may be back," Ki said. Ki now revealed to Jessica and Firesky that Etting was Laslo. Neither was completely surprised. "I'd think that we would be better off moving away from this camp and toward this Roaring Slope."

"The Chinee's right," Jake said. "Joe—get Hal, then you bring down those horses you boys rounded up. Pronto! There's only six of 'em," he told Ki, "but we can double

129

up—it'll sure as hell beat walking."

"Roaring Slope?" Jessie asked Firesky. "Do you know where that is?"

"Yes. Once there was a mountain pueblo there. Built before the Apaches came to this land by a strange and very ancient people. Later we lived there in summer. Roaring Slope. We called it The Place of the Clouds."

Joe was back with another Sunset rider. They had the horses behind them and now Jake divided them up. Jessie and Firesky had one horse, a blue roan, wall-eyed, stubby; Ki and Nati another. "That'll make it cozy," Jake said sourly. He himself rode alone on a sorrel with a white blaze and white stocking.

The land was still warm when they rode out into the dark, jumbled high country. Behind them a thin tendril of fire still softly glowed against the dark earth, but it wouldn't be burning much longer. It had nearly reached the sand desert below and once it was there the fire would be snuffed out. Above, the pale three-quarter moon had shaken free of its sheer, smoky veil and glowed brighly, coldly, casting a sheen on the barren slopes.

"This gang of white men," Firesky said as he, Ki, and Jessie rode in line up the winding moonlit trail, "these cartel people—they will know we are coming, Jessie Starbuck?"

"Yes. I guess they will," she replied.

"They will be waiting up there somewhere. This man Jake—is he a fool as I believe?" Firesky asked.

Jessie considered it soberly. "No," she said at last, "I don't think he is a fool. He is hard to like, but I think he knows what he is doing."

"I hope so," Firesky said quietly. "I do hope so."

"Where did you learn your English, Firesky?" Jessie asked, leaning forward, her arms around his waist.

130

"On a reservation," he said and he would say no more about that.

The land grew sharper, more defined, taller, more crooked, eerie in the moonlight. Far below they could just see the white sand desert gleaming softly. Above were the ragged peaks surrounding Roaring Slope. The scent of cedar and pine drifted to them from upslope as the gentle wind began to gust and prod. It grew cooler. The small company was quiet. There were only the shifting of weary men in the saddles, an occasional sigh or groan, the soft whisper of the horses' hooves against the stone of the old trail they followed upward.

Ghostly cedar trees overhung the trail now and the canyon narrowed. A star gleamed in a notch in the hills before them. Jessica wanted to stretch her arms, to break into a yawn, but it would have been like violating a taboo even to move, to break the long deep silence of the night.

The small, dark army moved upward for another half hour before they emerged onto a grassy valley. Jessica Starbuck couldn't see them, but she could smell them. She could smell cattle in the darkness and she came alert, clutching the rifle she had carried across her lap with a firm right hand.

Firesky glanced at her and nodded. They could see their leader, Jake, hold up his hand and the short, dark column moved quickly into the trees lining the road.

They gathered around the Sunset foreman as the moon, larger now and coasting toward the western horizon, gleamed through the trees and illuminated Jake's face.

"I guess you all know we're right on top of 'em," Jake said. "But we can't ride in like this. Someone's gonna have to ride ahead and scout."

"I will . . ." Firesky began.

"Anyone but the Indian," Jake amended sharply.

"I am the best scout you will find here!" Firesky said, laughing with consternation.

"You think I'm going to let an Apache ride out of here and maybe bring back a pack of other Chiricahua, you're crazy. I'm keeping an eye on you, Firesky."

"Why?"

"Damn you, because the first indication I get that this is some kind of trick, the first sign of a pack of damned Apaches laying for us, you're going to die."

Firesky leaped toward Jake, but Joe tripped him and he went down. Jake started to kick at him, but Ki stepped in and held his arm, pulling him back.

"Let go of me, Chinee."

"I will go ahead and scout the valley," Ki told him.

Jake was breathing in deeply, rapidly. He looked at Ki with glazed eyes, which gradually cleared as he regained his composure. From the corner of his eye he noticed that the blonde had her rifle pointed in his direction.

"All right. Do it, Chinee—I reckon you'll be back. You wouldn't want to leave the little lady here alone, would you?"

"I will be back," Ki said tersely.

"All right. Charlie, get that redskin's weapons. Frisk him for a knife. Take the lady's rifle, too. All right, lady? You and the Indian are kind of close?"

Jessie looked at Ki and then at Firesky who was only now dragging himself to his feet. She turned over her rifle. What else was there to do? They would take it from her anyway unless she started firing—and that would mean the finish of it for all of them.

"Thanks, little lady," Jake said. His arrogance had returned as he found himself in charge of the situation once again. "Chinee—get on ahead and see what's happening. One hour, all right?"

"Yes, one hour," Ki agreed. Jessica could see that he was restraining himself with some difficulty; even a man with Ki's composure could be pushed but so far. He nodded to Jessica and then, afoot, started ahead through the trees, his movements nearly silent, his shadow blending with those of the weary pines. Firesky walked to Jessie and stood beside her, holding his ribs. He had fallen against a rock when they had tripped him and he thought that one rib at least had cracked. That was nothing new to Firesky, however; pain was an unfortunate but constant part of his life.

"This Ki," the warrior asked Jessica, "he is good?"

"He is good. Very good."

Firesky nodded with satisfaction. "I thought so. I can see the warrior's movement in his body, the look in his eyes, the sound of it in his voice. He knows combat; he knows himself."

"He knows combat," Jessie agreed. "He knows himself, our Ki does."

Ki was hoping that he was good enough to do this job. He wove through the trees toward the faint scent of wood smoke he had detected on the wind. This excursion hadn't gone right from the start. Every time he and Jessie thought they were making progress, a new hitch developed. Just now they had the feud between Firesky and Jake to worry about.

Also, Ki realized, we have gained nothing on the cartel. Not manwise. If the cartel had lost a few men including Laslo, then the Sunset ranch had lost an equal number, and so at best they had remained where they had been—vastly outnumbered, without hope of reinforcements.

Ki slowed and crouched, moving forward with great caution through the mountain sage which now filled the gaps between the widely separated trees.

He could see fire.

Smoke rose from the chimney of a dilapidated stone house which might have been made hastily by the cartel men as shelter from the constant wind or perhaps was left from an earlier settler's attempt to ranch the valley where the weather was hard and the Apaches roamed.

Beyond the house the land rose in tiers, pines stippling the bluffs which would have been red in the sunlight but were a deep purple by the light of the fading moon, a huge, bulbous orange presence in the dark western sky.

On the bluffs Ki could see strange hollows and odd geometric shapes, angles and lines, planes nature could not have formed, and it was a time before he recalled what Firesky had said, that there were cliff dwellings on those bluffs where people had once lived, hunted, loved, worked, and died.

Ki's eyes were drawn by a movement on the dark valley floor. Two riders coming in slowly from the south, obviously at ease, apparently unaware that there had been a battle not far from this hidden place.

The cattle milled across the valley, dark, stolid, oblivious to the excitement they had been causing. Ki moved down closer to the buildings below. He had seen something there that intrigued him.

Beyond the corral was a makeshift corral of poles and green boughs, where the cartel soldiers' horses were kept. If those could be taken or set free to run, the numbers would no longer matter. The cartel people wouldn't to be able to do much fighting if they couldn't catch up with Jake, Ki, and Firesky.

Ki had two options—try it on his own or head back and

report. To go back seemed a waste of time. All they would probably do then would be to send a man—probably Ki— back to the very job he was now in a position to do. Besides, it wasn't all that long until dawn and once the sun rose there was no chance whatever of sneaking across the valley to the corral.

He started on.

Finding a dry wash cut into the valley floor, Ki slipped into it and worked his way up the winding watercourse toward the building and the corral. He heard horses nearby once, horses with riders—the creaking of saddle leather, the chinking of spurs was clear in the night's silence—and he lifted his head to see cartel soldiers slowly coming to the bunkhouse. It appeared they changed shifts at this time of the morning. Ki heard one of the men say something about coffee and eggs.

He kept his head low until they were past, watching them through a low stand of chia brush. When they were past, their dust slowly settling, Ki went on, glancing now and then toward the eastern horizon, dreading the first pale light of dawn which would make things difficult indeed, very difficult.

The dry wash swung away from his objective and Ki had to crawl up onto the flats and begin wriggling toward the corral. Fifty feet away a lantern went on in the cartel bunk-house, painting rectangles of dull yellow against the earth as it shined through the window.

A horse snorted and Ki halted, every muscle in his lean body poised, but he saw no one, nothing, only horses' heads silhouetted against the sky. He went on, moving silently, swiftly.

When he had moved to within twenty feet of the rails, he rose and worked his way toward the gate, a crude affair of rawhide ties and pine boughs. The horses inside the pen watched him with curious eyes. Ki moved slowly so as not to startle them.

He reached for the wire loop which held the gate shut, raised it, and swung the gate to him.

There was no sound that Ki could hear until the swishing of a heavy club through the air brought his head around, caused his arms to go up automatically in a cross-wrist block. But that was all too late. The club thudded off his skull and Ki went down, seeing the dark figure towering over him and beyond him faint stars swirling into the infinity of dark sky.

★
Chapter 13

"Where the hell is the Chink?" Jake demanded. He paced restlessly back and forth. "Don't tell me the bastard pulled out on us."

"That thought doesn't even deserve the dignity of a response," Jessica Starbuck snapped.

"Huh? Where the hell is the Chink, I said."

"He'll be back," Jessie said.

"He'd better damn well hurry—it's getting toward sunrise. I knew I shouldn't have sent him."

"If Ki can't do it, none of your people could have," Jessie commented, her irritation growing. She was leaning against a tree, rifle in hand. Firesky was crouched on the ground at her feet. Nati was looking nervously off into the distances, beginning to worry seriously about Ki now. He had been gone too long and they all knew it.

"I'll give him fifteen minutes," Jake said.

"And then what?" Firesky asked.

"And then we go in."

"Without having a scout's report on the enemy position?" Firesky said.

"We do what we have to do."

"It is suicide. It accomplishes nothing."

"Yeah? Got a better idea?"

"Not better perhaps," Firesky said with restraint, "but different. Let me go and find Ki."

"How do we know that's where he'd go?" Charlie asked. The barrel-shaped man was more than a little concerned. "You said yourself he's likely to go and bring his warriors back and take care of all of us."

"That's right." Jake said, "You stay, Apache."

"Then I'm going," Jessica announced, coming away from the tree. "I'm not leaving Ki out there, not knowing what's happened to him."

"No," Jake said, "no one goes. The Chinee's all right or he isn't. The more of us who go down there the better chance there is of losing everything."

"If they have Ki, then they already know we are up here."

Firesky added, "We still don't know the position of the soldiers of this cartel, where the cattle are, where their horses and guns are."

"Too much damn talk," Jake said abruptly. His nerves seemed to be giving out on him.

"We can't wait past sunrise," Charlie said.

"Shut up! I know it. Okay—it's like this—Firesky, Miss, get on down there if you want and find the Chinee."

"Jake, if you let this Apache go . . ." Charlie objected loudly.

"Shut up, I said! We've come this far with him. We trust

him or we don't. They're going down." He glanced to the east. "But if that sky starts to pale and you aren't back, just get out of the way because we're going to go in anyway."

"Jake, it's suicide."

"Charlie," Jake sighed, "shut up. It's for Champ Corson, for the brand. You're drawing fighting wages; it's damn soon time to earn them."

Jessica was smiling faintly. She said quietly to Jake, "Thank you."

"Sure, it's . . . hell," he growled, "I don't know what you're talking about. Do your job." Then Jake stalked away and Firesky watched him go.

"He is not so hard as he pretends," the Apache leader said with a kind of amazement.

"No. Nor are you," she said, kissing him. "There's no time to waste. Let's get going."

Nati had eased toward them, her eyes sharp with determination. "I will go, too."

Firesky said, "No! I would send you home if it were up to me, but it is not. You will not go with us, though."

"Jessica . . ." Nati pleaded but Jessie shook her head, agreeing with Firesky.

"Two of us is plenty. You wait right here. We'll bring him back. Don't you worry about that."

Nati wanted to say something, perhaps to argue, but after opening her mouth to speak she shook her head and clamped her lips shut, turning her back on them, walking slowly away into the trees.

"There isn't much time," Firesky said.

"No." And if they didn't get Ki out of there before Jake started shooting, he would be the first casualty of this battle. The cartel men wouldn't be reluctant to put a bullet through his head. "Let's go," she said, and they started through the trees, Jake watching them impatiently.

"Be ready," he told his men. "We go in at sunrise no matter what."

"Blind?" the man named Joe asked. "We won't know what we're up against."

"Blind. I'm taking it to them. Damn it—we've found them and now they're going to pay for taking from Sunset."

"There won't be much of a chance for the Chinee or the girl if we start it while they're down there."

"No, but I don't think they've got much of a chance anyway, do you? They've got the Chinee and they'll be waiting, watching. They'll take the woman, too. As for Firesky, they'll likely cut his throat and that's the best favor they could do us."

Joe turned away, tightening his cinch. Jake seemed to have been knocked crooked. He wasn't thinking straight. He just wanted to draw blood.

"A man could ride to the fort," Charlie said quietly. "A man could bring some soldiers back."

"In two days, maybe," Jake shouted. "Damn all—now you men want the army to do your fighting for you! This is Sunset and we do our own hunting."

And that was the final word on that. It wasn't going to do any good to protest that they were outnumbered, that if they didn't get a scouting report they were going to go in blind. Jake was going to burn some rifle ammunition and that was that.

The trouble was it was going to leave a lot of people dead on Roaring Slope and all of them weren't going to be cartel men.

It was still dark as Jessie and Firesky found the dry wash Ki had used. By the meager starlight the Chiricahua Apache could see where Ki's feet had broken down the bank as he slid into it.

Firesky jabbed a finger toward the distant horse corral, and Jessica, knowing Ki, understood. He would have seen the horses and gone after them, knowing that he could cripple the cartel's army in that way. Since the horses were still safely in the corral it was apparent that Ki had failed— and if he had failed then he was a prisoner . . . or dead.

Firesky went on silently, swiftly, Jessie at his heels, trying to still her labored breathing. Firesky was too quick for her. He seemed not to be exerting himself at all yet he flew across the ground, weaving through the brush in the bottom of the dry arroyo. He had a reason for hurrying—there was a pearly-gray glow along the eastern horizon above the hills where the cliff dwellings stood. Dawn was minutes away.

A cartel man loomed up suddenly in front of Firesky but the Apache didn't even slow down, let alone allow the man to speak, to threaten him with the rifle in his hands.

Firesky's knife flashed and buried itself in the warrior's throat and the Prussian, far from home, slumped to the dark earth to die quickly, silently.

They ran on.

At the end of the arroyo they could look back and see the corral from the back, see the cartel men crouched, looking northward, awaiting more infiltrators. Firesky lay beside Jessie, his arm on her back, his thigh touching hers, thrilling her even at this tense moment.

"There," he whispered, rolling toward her, breathing into her ear. His finger indicated a small outbuilding, a woodshed perhaps where a man with a rifle, or perhaps a shotgun, stood guard.

Firesky's instincts were right. There was no purpose at all that Jessie could conjure up for that guard to be outside the woodshed unless someone—Ki—was being held inside it.

"He's alive then," Jessie said so softly that not even

Firesky could have heard her. He was alive, had to be or they wouldn't have had a guard there at all. They wouldn't need to stand watch over a corpse.

"What now?" Jessie asked. It was growing light quickly, too quickly. There wasn't time to formulate a safe, sure plan—if there ever were such a thing.

"I will distract them," Firesky said and he started to rise. Jessie pulled him back.

"You'll what!"

"They will see me and come to me. I will distract them. Take your rifle and eliminate the guard at the woodshed."

"Oh, no you don't. I love Ki, but I won't have one man kill himself so that another can survive. Ki would be the first to object."

"There is no other way."

"We'll find another. *I'll* distract them. They won't shoot me, will they?"

"*No*, Jessica," Firesky said firmly.

"Why not? You can put an arrow into that guard and spirit Ki away."

"A fine plan! And what would Ki say to *this* idea?"

"It's got to be one or the other," Jessie said. Time was growing short and there didn't seem to be any brilliant ideas forthcoming. "I'm going," Jessie announced after Firesky's long silence, and she actually started up out of the arroyo before the sound of gunfire caused her to drop back to the ground.

Jake was attacking.

The sun had risen, bursting into red and yellow fire beyond the saw-toothed ridge. A line of gold limned the horizon, and as if the sun had lighted a fuse, touched powder, and turned the peaceful mountain meadow into a battleground, the first flush of color had started the guns to firing.

"Now," Firesky said and he nearly pushed Jessica on her way. All of the cartel men were rushing toward the bunkhouse to get their weapons or to receive their orders. It didn't matter which. Meanwhile Firesky made his dash toward the corral as Jessica stumbled to the woodshed left temporarily unguarded as the cartel thug, shaken by the sounds of battle ran toward the bunkhouse, leaving Ki alone temporarily.

Firesky didn't waste time with the gate. He kicked the flimsy poles from their moorings and began herding the horses from the corral. The distant shots, now growing nearer helped to speed the horses on their way. From the bunkhouse a shout of alarm preceded a dozen rapid shots aimed in Firesky's direction.

All of these missed. Firesky was behind the horses, and though one bullet seemed to tag horseflesh, none reached him.

Meanwhile Jessie had reached the woodshed, hurriedly opened the wooden latch and kicked in the door. Ki was crouched there, ready. He laughed out loud as he saw Jessica silhouetted against the dawn sky, rifle in her hands.

"Let's go," she said. "Fun's over."

Ki emerged into the morning light, patting his pockets, assuring himself that the cartel men hadn't found his *shuriken* nestled in their special pockets. They hadn't, and as a thug in chaps and red flannel shirt appeared from behind the woodshed, Ki sent one of the razor-edged throwing stars unerringly into the man's heart. He went down instantly, twitching violently, leaking blood against the dry grass.

They heard the sound of approaching horses and Jessie and Ki looked to the west. It was Firesky between two horses, holding their manes as he half ran, half rode toward the woodshed. A barrage of gunshots followed him but the attacking Sunset riders from the east caused them to break off their concentrated fire. Firesky arrived in one piece, two sturdy bay horses flanking him.

"The fight," he shouted, "How does it go?"

They couldn't answer the Apache. They could, in fact, see little of the battle except the smoke from the rifles in the bunkhouse.

"Jake's outnumbered, but his people are mounted—with any luck . . ."

"There is no luck," Firesky said. "Look!"

Their heads swung northward. A group of mounted men had burst from the woods—the people Laslo had left behind at the night camp, apparently. They came in with weapons barking, thundering down on Jake and his people. Jessie could see Jake now, see the Sunset riders break away from the cattle herd which was beginning to mill nervously and even then to stampede.

In a moment the herd was in a wild flight toward the north, Jake and the Sunset riders fleeing eastward. There was a cheer from the bunkhouse and a dozen cartel men emerged to fire at the retreating Sunset crew. Jessie saw Charlie go down, saw Joe double up. She lifted her rifle to her shoulder and sent six rounds of .44-40 ammunition into the pack of cartel thugs. With a *yip* they scooted back into the bunkhouse, leaving one man behind, being followed by another man who was limping heavily.

The window on the near side of the bunkhouse was torn out and they began to fire toward the bunkhouse. Simultaneously the incoming cartel riders, hearing the guns, swung toward the woodhouse.

"That's it," Ki shouted. "Let's go and now."

They tossed Jessie bodily onto the back of the stocky bay and Ki leaped up behind her, heeling the horse sharply so that it jumped forward, reaching its stride in three long bounds.

Glancing back, Jessie saw Firesky clinging to the far side of the second horse, using it for a shield as they raced southward, away from the ranch.

The mounted cartel men were in pursuit and they weren't hesitant about using the weapons they carried. Shot after shot rang out, but the distance opened up between the fresh horses and the hard-ridden cartel mounts, and in another few minutes they were out of gunshot range, riding free across the dry, rocky flats.

They found Joe's body a quarter of a mile on along a dry wash. His horse stood there looking down at the body and Ki took up the reins, adjusting cinches and stirrups. A little way on, as they walked their horses into the dry uplands, they found another Sunset rider, a Mexican whose name Jessie never knew.

He gave us his guns to Firesky as well as the little ammunition he had.

They rode silently after that, upwards always, toward the strange cliffs which cut nearly geometric figures against the sky, toward the ancient cliff dwellings.

Once from atop a ridge where the wind blew savagely, shearing off the scraggly cedar that grew there, they looked back toward the valley below. Everyone was exhausted. They let the horses blow and they stepped down to rest. Jessie saw them first and she pointed.

"There they go, Ki. Damn it all," she said.

She was mad enough to spit. Ki appeared composed but he knew that they had lost another vital round in this battle. The cattle that had been held at Roaring Slope were being moved out by the cartel hands—being taken to the west, into the hills and beyond that onto the flats on the California side.

"There's nothing we can do about it," Ki said.

"No, nothing at all." The herd was gone and that was

it. The cartel had won again. "If only Jake hadn't gotten so impatient."

"It wouldn't have mattered, Jessie. We just didn't have enough men."

"Others . . ." Firesky pointed. There were still a dozen cartel men in the valley. And they weren't left behind to round up the strays.

"They want us, I think," Jessica said. "If there's a chance of putting us out of business whoever is in charge would be anxious to do it."

"I think you're right," Ki said. He looked to the hills, to the northern skies which now began to clot with blue-black thunderheads as the wind continued to build. "It looks like rain."

Firesky nodded. "It will rain. Very hard."

"What do we do? The horses are exhausted," Jessie said.

"Do what you must," Ki said, "find shelter."

"What do you mean, Ki?" Firesky asked. "Where are you going?"

"Nati," Ki said, "she's still back there somewhere. I'm not going to ride off and leave her."

"She is Apache," Firesky said. "She will be all right."

"I'm not leaving her."

"No, if you want us . . ." Jessie began.

"I want you to stay here. We've at least got you out of danger for the time being." Ki's voice was unusually strict. The strain was beginning to tell on him, perhaps. Or the concern he felt for Nati.

"Yes, Ki," Jessie said. There was a hint of a smile in her tone, amusement at being bossed by him, but Ki didn't hear it.

"I will take Jessie to the cliff dwellings," Firesky said. "No one can get at us there. I know places where no man can come unless I allow it."

Ki looked to the cave houses, some four stories high, and he nodded. "Good. I will return when I can. When you see me signal, wave a cloth."

"Ki . . ." Jessica said.

"I am going back," Ki said, firmness in his voice. Firesky might have been absolutely correct—Nati might have simply remained where she was and, having seen that the battle was going the wrong way, turned, and started back toward Bowie and the reservation.

Or it could be that the cartel had her. She would be unique among them. She was a woman.

Ki started off again, down the long canyon, seeing the cartel thugs riding toward them two miles off. By cutting through the forest below and over the low hogback ridge, he could find another route, one which left him concealed, so he started that way, glancing back only once as Firesky and Jessica started toward the cliff dwellings, toward safety— or apparent safety.

Then Ki returned his gaze to the wooded hills, to the desert beyond, to the gathering storm to the north. If that storm drifted in, it would cause heavy rain in the mountains, flash floods in the canyons. It could leave them virtually cut off from the rest of the world, making travel nearly impossible.

But it could cover movements as well, conceal and camouflage them, and drive their pursuers to seek cover. So Ki watched the clouds and he hoped, hoped for the wildest torrent he had ever seen.

★

Chapter 14

They climbed a long stretch of steps carved into the soft, yellow-gray sandstone. The centers of the steps were concave, worn down by thousands of footsteps, women bringing in maize, men going out to hunt, children playing. Jessie looked up at the cliff dwellings above her. There were ancient eyes there, windows and doors staring bleakly out at the desert beyond as if from a yellow skull.

Glancing down, Jessica saw the earth fall away sharply. It was three hundred feet to the base of the cliff. The cliff dwellings were eminently defensible. That was the reason the ancient cave inhabitants had built here, in this way. No army of attacking Indians was going to charge up the narrow steps.

The wind was gusting up the canyon. The sounds it made in the windows and the doors of the caves was eerie and

149

ancient. A people seemed to chant from out of their graves.

"Here, Jessie," Firesky said as they achieved a narrow ledge.

Jessie stood panting, looking upward. There was a ladder some thirty feet high leading to a second ledge where a door had been carved into stone.

"That ladder must be two hundred years old," she said dubiously, looking at the ancient rawhide lashings, the gray wood of the poles. "Will it hold us?"

"Yes. Go first. I will catch you if you fall," Firesky said.

"I hope so." Jessie wasn't enthusiastic about the project, but there wasn't much choice. They weren't going back and they weren't going to spend the night in the open on that ledge—not with those rain clouds drifting in. She started up the ladder.

Firesky braced the ladder and watched her climb, and though his mind was concerned with her safety, his eyes couldn't help lingering on the way her hips swayed as she climbed, on the firm beautiful bottom encased in those tight jeans and Firesky felt a pulsing begin in his groin.

Jessie disappeared over the ledge and she turned to call back, "All right. Come on up."

Firesky began to climb, the wind twisting around him now, beginning to shriek and wail ominously.

When he reached the ledge he found that Jessie had moved into the cave house and was gathering the nests of several packrats—bark and twigs and straw and making the foundation for a fire. Outside thunder rumbled distantly.

Firesky watched her bend over and puff at the fire, stretching those jeans tighter yet. He watched her purse her lips, watched the expression of concentration as she puffed on the fire, bringing it to life, and he knew that he was giving himself away, that he had developed a hungry erection, a thrusting bulge beneath the trousers he wore.

150

Jessie turned, looked questioningly at him then lowered her gaze to his crotch. She smiled, stretched out her hands, and waited on her knees for Firesky to come to her.

He went to Jessica as the fire flared up and illuminated the dark, ancient interior of the cavern, the cavern which had been a home, a place of refuge until... until what? Until plague or invasion or famine?

Jessica's hands rested on Firesky's legs and she smiled as she looked up at him, her lips parting, her honey-blond hair glowing softly in the firelight. She rubbed his erect shaft gently, deep enjoyment reflected in her eyes, and Firesky, feeling the warming glow of sexual excitement within, shrugged out of his clothes, scattering them everywhere.

Jessie also undressed. By firelight she was a goddess in bronze and ivory, perfectly formed, breasts full, pink budded, slightly uptilted, anxious for his lips. Firesky went to his knees and kissed her inside her thighs, his fingers creeping up to enter her as she sighed and spread her legs slightly, her hand resting on his head.

She sank to her knees as well and Firesky, kissing her, moved to her so that they met, Jessica's breasts flattening themselves against his hard chest as his hands reached around and clenched the half globes of her ass.

Jessie laughed, bit him on the shoulder lightly, and lifted herself, grasping his rock-hard pole, guiding it into her inner recess, laughing with joy as he sank to the hilt in her warmth.

The fire was warm, the wind outside blustering and cold. Jessie leaned back and Firesky kissed her throat, her breasts, as an irresistible trembling began in his loins, and Jessie swayed and rolled against him, nipping at his shoulders, his earlobes, his lips.

He clung to her, his head on her shoulder, feeling her begin to alter, to grow softer, sweeter, more slack against him, feeling her tense and then relax, hearing her soft sighs

151

as he filled her with his warm rush.

They remained that way, facing each other on their knees, feeling the glow which settled over them intensify and then slowly wane to a pleasant memory.

Then, with the fire burning low they reluctantly separated and half dressed, they scavenged the cave dwelling for wood, finding some ancient collapsed pole beams in another room. Pole which had held the artificial adobe ceiling in place.

"They made the ceiling lower," Jessie said. "Look up there. The cave roof is so high that they could never have heated it." She peered up into the dark vastness, believing she saw a distant point of light. It was difficult to be sure. She had no desire to climb up and see.

"Come on," she said and Firesky helped her carry back the old, broken poles to the fire. The smoke and flames rose toward a vent in the ceiling, the smoke vanishing, merging with the clouds overhead. It would not be seen on this day.

An hour later as Jessie stood on the ledge watching Firesky pull up the ancient ladder, it began to rain. A few huge silver drops spattered the ground and within moments it was a torrent. They ran for the mouth of the cave, where they stood together watching lightning arc across the canyon, listening to the deep rumbling of thunder as the rain sheeted down.

Firesky watched the woman with the green eyes, her hair damp, her blouse wet, showing the contour of her pink breasts. There was concern in her eyes.

"He will be all right," the Apache said.

"Yes. Ki is always all right. Nothing can happen to Ki."

"No. Nothing can happen."

Jessie nodded. Nothing could happen, except *damn it* he was out there alone in this weather searching for Nati while the cartel searched for him. And if they found him this time there would be no mercy, no probation, no concern about holding him for questioning. It was too late for that with Laslo gone, with the stolen herd gone. They would have only two thoughts in mind. Find Jessica Starbuck and eliminate her. Find Ki and eliminate him.

"Nothing can happen," she said again and it convinced neither her nor Firesky. The wind thundered down the long canyon and the rain came in again, harder yet.

Ki lifted his eyes to the storm. It rumbled across the world, causing the trees surrounding him to shudder and moan as the rain hammered down and lightning slashed bright seams across the tumbling gray sky.

He could see nothing beyond the rain and the trees, hear nothing above the roar and crackle of the storm. He walked through the pines now, leading his horse. There were cartel people around him somewhere—how he knew this, he couldn't have said, but he *felt* their presence. He could only hope that they could not feel his.

"Where is Nati?"

That question plagued him. He was nearly to the spot where he had last seen the Apache woman; but although he had extracted from her a promise to remain there, he couldn't seriously expect her still to be there. Since that time a battle had begun, a storm had broken, Ki had left and vanished in the hills.

"Where would she go?" he asked himself. "Where?"

The reservation was impossibly distant. She had had no idea of where Ki might be except on the Roaring Slope which now was beginning to live up to its name as the wind bellowed across the high valley.

He bowed his head to the storm and went on, through the shuddering pines with the rain lashing down. He then saw, or thought he saw, a small red eye winking brightly through the storm. A campfire? But when he stopped to try to pinpoint the location he couldn't find it again and he had to walk on, shivering with the cold.

Lightning struck near at hand and the sulfuric scent of it flooded Ki's nostrils as the flash sent him recoiling. The following thunder rattled his eardrums, temporarily deafening him.

And then, quite magically, as if she had been delivered by the lightning bolt, had ridden it down out of the tumultous sky, Nati was there.

"Nati?" Ki blinked, doubting his own senses, but she wasn't some being fabricated by his own imagination, his own wants. She rushed to him, clung to him, wet and cold, her hair flattened down across her face. Ki kissed her through the veil of hair, finding her mouth warm, eager.

"I had hoped..." she began. "I thought they had killed you. You didn't come back and then Jessica and Firesky did not return, and then at dawn Jake rode into the cattle camp. I saw only a part of the fight, enough to know that he had lost."

"You should have returned to Bowie, to the reservation," Ki told her, stroking her head, kissing her rain-jeweled forehead.

"How could I, not knowing what had happened to you, Ki?" she asked with surprise. "What would you have me do, walk away from it all?"

"No. I did not think you would. That's why I came looking for you."

"Jessica and Firesky?"

"They are all right. They are in the cliff dwellings," Ki replied, nodding toward the south.

"Good. I was worried..."

"And now you no longer have to worry."

"No? I am still worried, Ki. What about the people on

154

the reservation, those we started out to help? We haven't done well, have we? We have failed and now there is nothing at all we can do."

"We will see. We will discuss it," Ki said. "Get up on the horse now and let's get out of the rain."

The voice from the trees caused Ki to freeze as he started to swing Nati up onto the horse's back.

"I wouldn't worry about getting wet, Ki, you're not going to feel the rain."

Slowly Ki turned his head toward the man. There were two of them, one a step or two behind. Both had drawn their Colts. They were cartel men and they knew what they wanted . . . Ki's death.

Ki slowly released Nati and stepped aside.

"I told you if we followed the squaw she'd lead us to them, Bret. I knew she was with 'em."

"All right. Shut up. Spread out a little. *Ki*—that is your name, isn't it? I ought to know. I heard about you plenty of times from Laslo. What did you do to Laslo anyway?"

Ki didn't answer. His eyes shuttled from point to point, trying to find some way out of this. Nati was five feet to his right. Before him were the two gunmen. The background was very dark, tall trees rising into the gray storm as the rain plummeted down. Distantly lightning struck a brilliant image against the sky.

"Hold those hands a little higher, Ki . . . not any closer, you damned fool!" he said to his cohort. "He can break your back with a kick. Isn't that right, Ki?"

"I wouldn't mind trying," Ki said tightly.

"Oh, he can be funny at a time like this. Good, very good, Ki. He's got them throwing stars in his pockets; watch his hands. If he makes a move, kill him."

"Kill him now! What're we waiting for?"

That one was nervous. Bret shot him a scornful glance.

"He knows where the Starbuck woman is. Don't you understand what that means? If we find her and capture her—or kill her—we'll be set for life. Don't you know what the reward is on that bitch?"

"All right. Let's get on with it. What do you want me to do? Shoot off his toes one by one?"

"No." Bret looked at Nati and smiled thinly. "Let's shoot *hers* off, and if that don't work maybe we can come up with something a little more interesting."

"Bastard!" Nati spat and she leaped forward, clawing at Bret's eyes. Bret stepped back in surprise and Ki moved.

The other thug's eyes were momentarily distracted and Ki's sharp side-kick snapped the wrist bone of the gunman's arm. With a howl of pain he went to his knees holding his wrist.

Ki started toward Bret, but he was too late, too slow. Bret hurled Nati aside and his gun came up. The hammer was back and Ki was ten feet from him. Bret's mouth parted in a thin smile and he started to squeeze off his shot.

He was just a hair too slow. The second gun spoke from the woods and as Ki watched in astonishment Bret was slammed back into a pine tree, his gun dropping from his hand, his face going blank and pale as blood seeped from his lips.

Jake strode forward reloading his weapon.

"How's things, Ki?"

"Jake!"

"What're you going to do with the other one?" the Sunset foreman asked, nodding at the thug with the broken wrist.

"Let him go."

"Sure? He'll be back." Jake holstered his Colt and wiped back his dark, stringy hair. He wore no hat, no coat. The rain was driving down still around them. They had to speak up to be heard above the downpour.

"Let him go. He won't return." Ki yanked the man to his feet and he howled with pain as the wrist bone grated together. "I *could* break your back, you know."

The cartel man went as pale as the bloodless Bret. "Please, Ki . . . Mister Ki . . ."

"Get going, now."

"Sure, my horse . . ."

"I got your horses," Jake said, "you just start walking."

"In this rain!"

"If you want, you can stay here and be nice and cozy with Bret there. He don't feel the rain—isn't that what you were telling Ki?"

The cartel hand looked at Bret, at Ki, and then he started walking away through the deep woods, the rain hammering down. It was the smartest thing he had done in a long while.

"There a place to get out of this?" Jake asked.

"Yes. Get the horses. Jessie and Firesky are at the cliff dwellings. We'll all be safe there. Safe and dry."

He hoped.

It wasn't going to be all that easy. Jake turned and started away and then stopped and stood stock still. He started to draw his gun, but it would have been a waste of time. He just backed up to stand beside Ki as they came out of the forest, dozens of them, all armed, all wanting their blood.

The Apaches had them completely surrounded.

★
Chapter 15

Ki glanced at Nati and started forward. The Apache with the yellow and black paint on his face fired his rifle, the bullet singing past Ki's head, slamming into the tree behind him, tearing a fist-sized chunk of bark from it as Ki's horse reared up in fright and danced away.

"Fool!" Nati shrieked. "What are you doing? Don't you know that this man is a friend of Firesky?"

"Firesky has no friends who are not Apache."

"Then you do not know Firesky," Nati spat. "This man is his friend. And so am I." She stretched the point a little indicating Jake, "And so is this white man."

"Shut your mouth woman! Who are you? Who asked you to speak your lies."

"They are not lies. Ask Firesky yourself!"

"We will ask him when we reach the ranch."

"He is not there. He is at the cliff dwellings of the ancient ones."

"With all his white friends," the leader of the war party jeered.

"With one very good one," Nati answered quietly.

There was a brief conference among the Apaches. Their leader was an impatient man, but cooler heads pointed out that if they were friends of Firesky they could do them no harm.

"Firesky has no friends like these."

"If he is at the cave dwellings we can find out soon enough—it isn't that far."

"And what if someone else is waiting there for us? White men, soldiers perhaps?"

"Then," the second man shrugged, "we fight. We kill the hostages and fight as we would fight them no matter where we encountered them."

"All right. Let it be so, but I do not like it."

Nati had already translated the import of the Apache exchange and Ki and Jake breathed a little easier though Jake tensed when they reached for and took his pistol. He felt just a little less secure without it on his hip.

"Bring their horses," the man with the yellow and black paint commanded and it was done. Then, with the Apaches surrounding them, they rode southward again, toward the bluffs which were lost in the swirling mass of cloud as the desert storm raged on.

They approached with caution and with some apparent trepidation, but Firesky himself appeared on the ledge above them and called out.

"Walking Fox! Come up, my friend. And Ki! Nati!" The Apache lifted both arms briefly. "We have had good luck."

And then to Walking Fox's astonishment Jessica Starbuck emerged from the cliff dwelling and stood, Firesky's arm around her, watching as they climbed the steps to the ledge.

"Ki!" Jessie came to him and hugged him, taking Nati's hand as well. Jake stood to one side like a schoolboy at a dancing party. The man with the yellow and black paint—Walking Fox—clasped Firesky's hand and forearm and the two Apache leaders held a hurried conference, Firesky telling the dubious Walking Fox about the episodes of the last few days, Walking Fox reporting on the raids the war party had conducted.

"And now what is there to be done?" Walking Fox asked when they were through speaking, when the party had moved inside to warm themselves around the fire. "Do we go home to rest, to prepare for our next raid? Do we expect Major Neilsen's soldiers? Do we flee again to the mountains?"

"I don't know what to do now," Firesky said. He looked to Jessie Starbuck.

"I do. And now it can be done," she said.

"I don't understand you, Jessie."

"We find Champ Corson."

"The white rancher?" Walking Fox exclaimed.

"The white rancher. We find Champ Corson and we make sure that the herd he's bought in Mexico gets to the Apaches on the reservation," she said.

"What do we care about the reservation Indians?" Walking Fox said passionately. "Women who would not help us fight."

"I care," Firesky said.

"I know this. It is foolishness though, Firesky. Forgive me, but it is."

"Nevertheless, it is so."

"Why does this Corson need help? He has hired men with him, no doubt. Why should we help him? We would be lucky if his cowboys did not shoot us as well," Walking Fox said.

"He needs the help," Jessica said. "The cartel knows he's coming up with a herd of cattle. They're anxious to cause trouble down here, anxious to snatch all the beef they can. You can be sure that there are enough people left behind to hit that herd and take it from Champ."

"Perhaps they do not know where he has gone."

"Laslo knew. He would have told his men. Yes, they know, and you can bet the cartel is after that herd. I don't know what we could have done about it before, but I know now—we've got fifty Chiricahua warriors here. That's an army. We can do it, and we have to—it's the last chance for the reservation Indians, for the reservation system in Arizona. If those people get hungry enough to break off the Bowie post, a lot of men, women, children on both sides are going to die. And that's not war, that's just tragedy."

Finished, she looked at Firesky whose decision it was to make. He closed his eyes briefly and then, backlighted by the bright fire, he said, "We ride. Now. We will find Champ Corson and help him bring the cattle through to Fort Bowie."

Walking Fox was furious. "To do this is to aid the enemy!"

"To do this," Firesky replied softly, "is to aid the people, the Apaches who hunger. Do not argue with me now, Walking Fox. I have decided." He got to his feet and raising his voice, said, "We ride, my warriors. Eat hurriedly, for we ride in minutes."

Jessie was on her feet now, snatching up her rifle. Firesky put a hand on her arm. "No, there is no need for you to go along, Jessie. It may be dangerous."

"Sure, it may be, but if you think I'm going to miss out on this, you're greatly mistaken. Ki?"

"We will ride with you," Ki said with resolution.

Jake said, "That's my brand—I'm going as well. Have that savage over there give me back my handgun."

162

Nati was also preparing to leave. She shrugged, "I should sit here alone and wonder and listen to the lies of the wind? No. I will go. I want to see these cattle. I want to see them delivered; I want to see the joy on the faces of the hungry."

Firesky sighed and looked to the heavens, but he said nothing.

No one argued. There wasn't time to argue. They had to leave and now. Those who couldn't keep up would be left behind. Somewhere on that desert Champ Corson was driving a herd northward; somewhere an army of cartel men would be waiting to steal the herd, to murder Corson and his men, to fatten the cartel's purse and prod a thousand innocent Indians into a war they couldn't win.

They rode.

It was storming heavily for the first three or four miles as Firesky led the band of Apaches, Ki, Jessie and Nati down the red canyon on the far side of the bluffs. He took them out onto the desert where the rain lessened but the wind seemed to take up the slack, gusting against them, flinging rain and sand at once into their faces. They rode south.

"Four men have gone ahead," Firesky expalined to Jessie, shouting over the roar of the wind. "They will spread out like this." His fingers described a fan. "They will find Champ Corson."

And Jessie thought: *if* he had made it this far, anywhere near this far, *if* the cartel hadn't already ridden down upon the Sunset owner, killing his people, running his herd away to join the other stolen ones on their way to the coast.

A gap appeared between the shifting clouds and through that gap Jessie saw sundown approaching. The sky was dark purple and dull red. The desert was endless, flat, dark, and gray beneath the roof of clouds.

Suddenly they saw a rider coming in. Apache, he was,

and coming hard. Their heads came up expectantly and they whipped their horses on even faster as the scout, waving his hand, charged toward them from out of the swirl of the storm.

He reined up his exhausted pony minutes later. "I saw them. One hour. Toward the Carrizo Gorge," the scout panted, pointing behind him.

"The cattle?"

"They have them. Hidden in the gorge so that the storm will not stampede them."

"The other whites, these cartel people?" Nati asked interrupting.

"I did not see them. But I saw their sign. Many horses. Many men moving south."

"White men?"

"White men, yes. Their ponies wore shoes."

Firesky glanced at Jessie. "I think we'd better keep riding, riding hard."

"Yes." The wind was whipping her hair around her intent face with its green eyes which gazed anxiously southward. "We can't lose those cattle, Firesky, we just can't."

"We won't," the Chiricahua leader said with determination. "Let us ride. Swiftly."

They started on again and the wind grew colder as the night settled in. The horses stumbled with exhaustion as their riders forced them to run on. The sky had cleared slightly so that they could make out pointing stars from time to time through the thick clouds. Around them on the desert, pools of water left by the storm shimmered dully. They would be gone by morning; the world would be dry and barren again.

"How far to Carrizo Gorge?" Jessica shouted to Firesky. They had been riding an hour at least, she was sure of that. It seemed like many hours.

"There," Firesky said and he pointed, and as if he had caused it all with his pointing finger the night detonated, becoming fire and sound and confusion. The guns in Carrizo opened up and the sound rolled toward the approaching Apaches.

"Now. They are attacking now!"

"Faster," Ki said although his mind was concerning itself with another problem—how were the Apaches to know which whites to kill? How would Corson's men know that the Apaches were not a part of the enemy force? He looked to Firesky who nodded as if to say "I know."

"You've got to let me go ahead," Ki said. "I've got to find Corson."

"No!"

"Yes. There'll be terrible, useless bloodshed if someone doesn't tell him what's happening."

"There's no time."

"There has to be time."

"You can't get through to Corson—if he's alive—they'll shoot you, too."

"I am going to go ahead," Ki said, and from the tone of his voice it was obvious that there was no argument which would sway him.

"All right." Firesky began to slow his horse, holding up his hand to stop those behind him. They were within a quarter of a mile of the battle. Shots echoed from the Carrizo Gorge and the muzzle flashes were clearly evident, like hundreds of matches briefly flaring up and then being snuffed out.

"Ki . . ." Jessie said. He glanced at her and she just shook her head. He heeled his horse and rode ahead alone toward the sounds of the guns.

The gorge was a dark maw against a darker background. Ki started up the gorge and then veered off to the right into

165

the brush which grew along the walls of the canyon.

The guns were very near now and twice Ki heard the startled whinny of a wounded horse, once the pained curse of a man presumably struck by a bullet.

He saw the herd suddenly, Mexican longhorns. They were excited, ready to run, confused. They were trapped between the guns of Corson's men and those of the cartel. Ki could feel the heat rising from the animals, see a thousand eyes in the starlight.

He left his own horse and started forward afoot, needing to find Champ Corson.

A cartel man was suddenly in front of him, and Ki kicked him in the throat, leaping over the body to rush on, fighting his way through the brush while the battle raged in the darkness below.

Ki found himself on a narrow shelf of stone. Below him was a watercourse, and after the brief, hard rain it gleamed silver with the stream it carried. Ki hesitated a moment, and then leaped, and landed standing in the ankle-deep water. He lurched forward to stumble on toward the cattle camp still clearly marked by their cookfire.

He could see the combatants now, firing from Champ Corson's camp and from horseback across the gorge. Ki shouted out above the thunder of the guns.

"Hello!"

Predictably he drew fire. Three rapid shots as Ki hugged the ground. He cried out again.

"Who's out there?" came a return cry.

"Ki! Tell Champ Corson I'm here. I want to come in."

It was only minutes but it seemed an interminable wait as the cowboy scooted across the camp and sought out the Sunset boss before returning.

"All right," the cowboy shouted, "Come in! Hands real high."

The guns crackled constantly from the other side of the camp. Ki went in with his hands very high, moving swiftly. When he got there he found Champ Corson waiting.

"Ki, what in hell are you doing here? Where's Jessica and Etting? Where in hell's Jake?"

"It would take a long time to tell you all of it, Champ, and we haven't got the time. Listen to me—we have these people beaten."

"Looks like it," the cowboy who had taken those shots at Ki said sourly.

"We do. We've only got to do as I say."

"Namely?" Champ asked apprehensively. They all ducked reflexively as a bullet flew past their heads.

"Let them have the herd," Ki said.

"Let them what!" Champ looked ready to burst. "Anything but that. Ki, you know what I've gone through to bring cattle to Bowie. If you think . . ."

"Champ, you've got to trust me. They can't get anywhere. We've got people at the mouth of the gorge who will cut them down."

"People?" Champ's eyes narrowed. "What people? My people?"

"No."

"Who then, damn it? The army?"

Ki hesitated. To tell the cattleman that it was Firesky was probably unwise. Yet he had to convince Champ to let the cartel take the cattle—it was the only way to separate the Sunset riders from the Apaches and avoid accidental killings.

"Who, Ki? You know me, you think I'll just let those cattle go if you don't tell me?"

And so Ki, swallowing hard, did. Champ Corson erupted. "Firesky! Damn it all—if this isn't the worst joke I've ever encountered. Its the damndest piece of craziness in Arizona

167

history. I'll give you fifteen seconds, Ki—you tell me just why I should go along with this madness."

"Because," Ki said simply, "It's your only chance. Firesky wants to feed his people on the reservation. So do you."

"I hate that bastard."

"I don't suppose he cares for you. That's why I'm telling you—stay here in the gorge."

"Ki..." Champ Corson looked deep into Ki's eyes and he saw something there that persuaded him. "If this is wrong, Ki, damn all, I'll..." He couldn't finish the sentence. He spun away angrily. The cowboy grabbed at his arm.

"Mr. Corson, Mr. Corson, this is crazy!"

Champ Corson shook him off. "Hold your fire! Hold your fire, boys—let 'em take the herd. Let 'em go!"

It was a long while before Corson could get everyone to cease firing and then in the stunned silence that followed they stood and watched and listened as the herd they had fought for was driven from the gorge and out onto the desert flats.

Corson looked at Ki, and he looked old, very old as he worked his jaw soundlessly and shook his head in quiet despair. Riding a borrowed horse, Ki started back toward the mouth of the gorge on the heels of the herd. He hadn't reached it when guns began to speak again, this time from Firesky's position, and Ki rushed on, hoping, hoping.

It was an uneven battle—the Apaches had had position on the cartel men and they had known the rustlers were coming. Yet the cartel men were determined, nearly desperate. Failure wasn't tolerated in the organization, and none of them wanted to die on the empty desert.

The guns roared. As Ki rode up, he saw the herd, aimless now, trample over two mounted cartel men who had tried to turn back into the face of the herd as Firesky's people rose out of the dark sands to cut them down.

Ki rode on, staying wide of the action. He only wanted to find Jessie and Nati, to assure himself they were all right. The battle, he believed, had a predetermined end. Firesky would win. They had done it, very nearly done it.

There was one last obstacle. A deadly obstacle. Where the man came from, how he identified Ki in the night, he didn't know, but he leaped from behind the boulders shouting:

"Ki! Hold up! Hold up!"

The *shuriken* was instantly in Ki's hand and it hummed through the space between them imbedding itself in the cartel thug's eye. He nodded to Ki and then fell on his face, dead.

Ki rode on and in another ten minutes he had found his friends. Jake stood there scratching his head. Jessica smiled brightly. Nati rushed to him and held him, clinging to Ki for a long, long while.

★

Chapter 16

Dawn came bright and showy. Crimson and gold poured across the eastern sky where a few long ragged clouds remained after the storm. The cattle, exhausted after their run, were bunched together on the flats, heads hanging, stoic now and ready to be moved.

"Sixteen head," Champ Corson said. The big man was standing beside his horse, thumbs hooked in the broad belt he wore. "That's all we lost—incredible."

"It beats me," Jake said again. He had repeated that sentence numerous times that morning. "It just beats the hell out of me. That damned Apache did what he said he'd do. Stopped the rustlers, left us the cattle, and took off for the hills—and the next time we see the son of a bitch he'll be wanting to make war again."

"You don't understand it?" Jessica asked.

"No, Miss, I'm damned if I do."

Jessie smiled to herself. Maybe she didn't understand it either, but she thought she did, thought she understood the noble motives of a noble man, a man of his people, one of royal blood despite the time and place, a true Apache prince. He had made his vow, carried through, and now he was gone. She had kissed him, held him, and then watched him ride off as sunrise created purple flame in the east.

"I don't understand it all either," Champ Corson said, "but I guess I don't need to. Let's get these cows moving, Jake. Let's head 'em into Bowie."

Jake nodded and walked off, chaps slapping as he led his horse toward the Sunset riders, who were gathered around the morning fire.

"It'll feel good," Champ told Ki and Jessie. "Good to take these steer right up that main street and watch all of them who said I was stealing beef swallow their words."

"It will feel good," Ki said, "to watch the hungry people eat."

Champ rubbed his chin, cocked his head to one side, and nodded. "You're right there, my friend." He slapped Ki on the shoulder and said, "Let's ride north and see just how good it does feel."

Champ turned then and walked off, calling to his men. Ki had the reins of his horse in his hand. Beside him was Nati. Jessie was there in body, but her eyes told them that her soul was far distant as she looked to the rugged hills above the desert.

"Ready, Jessica?"

"Ready." She sighed, smiled, and then was her old self. "Let's get to Bowie. We've got some business there yet."

The morning drive was long, but there were small amounts of water on the desert yet and the wind was cool. It was an easy drive yet each of them strained his eyes for the first

172

glimpse of the slovenly town and the time seemed to drag.

Shortly after noon the point man came riding in fast, halting before Champ Corson, his horse spraying sand. "There it is, boss," they heard him shout. "Damn me— we've made it!"

Then the cowboy let out a rebel yell which was echoed by other hands as they understood what lay ahead of them, that they had—on the third try—actually made it to Bowie with a herd. Champ Corson turned his head and blew his nose on his red bandanna.

Jessie found herself standing in the stirrups. It was true— now she could see the low, leaning, disreputable town, the fort and the reservation beyond, Apache Pass in the distance.

She slowly breathed in and then out again, settled in the saddle, glanced at Ki whose eyes were also fixed on the town, the fort.

An hour later they were pushing the steers past the wondering eyes of the army guards and onto the reservation proper where the Apaches came out en masse to stand by patiently, too silently for a long time until Jessica addressed them.

"I'm sorry this happened. It won't happen again—I'll see to it. You'll have your blankets and everything else you were promised. For now," she smiled, "feast! Fill your bellies!"

There was still no movement for a time, only deadly silence but then one young brave with a sharp knife and a will to eat moved in on a steer and bled it while others whooped and rushed to an old cooking pit to clear the rats and brush from it, to prepare it for the steer. It was roasting over a hot fire before Ki and Jessie started off the reservation with the Sunset riders.

"Ki," Nati said, "I will stay here. I want to be near the people."

"All right. I understand."

"Maybe you will be back. Maybe you will be back tonight."

She looked up at Ki who was mounted on his horse, her hand resting on his thigh. He smiled and bent low to kiss her.

"Maybe I will, Nati."

Champ Corson said, "I'm going to take the boys into Bowie and let them get good and drunk. They deserve it. Jessie—Ki—thanks. Maybe, if you've got anything to say about it, you could put in a word for me with the B.I.A. A contract as beef supplier would be mighty helpful toward getting myself and Sunset back on our feet."

"I wouldn't even consider recommending anyone else," Jessica said. Champ grinned, shook her hand with his huge paw, slapped Ki on the shoulder, and led his men off the reservation with a chorus of hoots and yips and yells.

"And now?" Ki asked.

"And now I'm going to do what I promised," Jessica Starbuck announced. "I'm going to see that this doesn't happen again. I'm going to get on that telegraph wire—assuming they've got it patched back together by now—and I'm going to talk to Washington again. I'm going to talk to General Ford and to Chris Wiley and everyone else I can think of and get this straightened around."

"The other Indian agencies have to be carefully scrutinized," Ki agreed. "The cartel has moved in and just because Laslo is gone, it doesn't follow that they'll move out."

"They'll move out," Jessica said. "If we have to do it ourselves, but after this scandal, I don't think we'll have to."

The telegraph wire was repaired but the telegrapher, a red-faced corporal refused to let Jessica use it.

"Major's orders, Miss. Standing order."

174

"Standing order, is it?" Jessie fumed. "We'll see about that, too!"

The corporal suddenly came out of his chair, jerking to attention. Jessie and Ki turned toward the open door to see Major Neilsen standing there. He came in slowly.

"What is it?" he demanded.

"I want to use the telegraph line."

"No. It's not for civilian use."

"In my capacity as Indian agent..."

"No. There's a key at the Crystal Falls stage stop. Sixty-five miles north," the major said smugly.

"Fine," Jessie said. She was fuming silently, quietly. Smoldering. "Then I'll use that wire. I'll use it to contact Senator Ned McCulloch and General Thomas Ford, both old friends of my father. I'll use it to contact Chris Wiley at the Department of the Interior. And I'll relate exactly what has happened here.

"I'll tell them that the commanding officer of this post wouldn't get up off his chair to try to solve the potentially bloody situation we had, rather he encouraged it, hoping for war..."

"Wait a damned minute, young lady!"

"I'll tell them that he knew things were wrong over on the reservation and wouldn't help; I'll inform them that although the commander of this post had an excess supply of beef cattle he wouldn't spare any, not even as a good will gesture to stem the bad feelings of the captive Apaches."

"I'm damned if you will. I..."

"I'll tell them in no uncertain terms that you refused to aid Ki and myself in an investigation of this problem, that in fact I believe you are an ineffective, belligerent, arrogant and perhaps incompetent officer. And believe me, Major, you'll never see a lieutenant-colonel's leaves."

"Now wait a minute. Listen to me, young lady..."

"Or—" Jessie offered, "you can let me use this key to send a message to B.I.A. asking for an investigation and clean-up of the reservation system, to ask for a skilled and incorruptible permanent agent to take over this particular reservation."

The major stood there turning different shades of purple, glaring at Jessica who didn't even blink. Finally he said in a barely controlled voice, "Young lady, I believe you are more intractable than Firesky himself. Damn all! Corporal!"

"Yes, sir!"

"See that the Indian agent here has access to the wire . . . on a priority basis." Then the major saluted limply and turned away. Perhaps only Ki saw it, or imagined it, but he thought there was a thin smile on Major Neilsen's face as he did so. However, when he exited, the door banged solidly, bringing dust down from the ceiling.

"Ready, Miss?" the telegrapher asked.

"Yes—yes, I'm ready. Here's the first message . . ."

Ki waited outside in the bright sunlight. The last of the clouds had drifted away. Jessica was inside, burning up the telegraph wires, bringing in supplies and intelligent help. There was some kind of flap in the ranks. Ki saw soldiers rushing toward the paddock, saddling their mounts, snatching up canteens and weapons.

Ki stopped one young trooper long enough to ask what was up.

"It's Firesky, sir. He's been spotted eighty miles to the north."

Which was in itself amazing since Ki had last seen the Apache miles to the south. He kept silent and watched as the cavalry patrol assembled, mounted, and rode out. He was aware of someone at his shoulder and he turned to see Jessie there.

"Finished?" he asked.

176

"I think so, hope so. What's up?" she asked, gesturing toward the soldiers. Ki told her. "One day, I expect," Jessie said. "One day they'll have him. We'll read about it. He's a soldier, Ki—he won't stop fighting."

"No. He won't. He believes he's right."

"One day then..." but her sentence broke off and she walked away. Ki didn't try to follow. Not then.

He rode instead toward the reservation. The sun was already beginning its slow descent. The western hills were purple. From the reservation came the sounds of singing, of drums, and the scent of roasting beef. Smoke rose into the sky, signaling plenty and well-being. Ki only hoped that Firesky could see the smoke in the southern hills and know what it meant.

She was there beneath the oaks and Ki went to Nati, who had changed into a clean white blouse, a skirt with a broad red stripe at the hem. She had washed herself with yarrow soap and treated her hair with fine, scented oil. She had put on her silver bracelets and silver necklaces with turquoise set into them and waited now, hands clasped, for the tall man who swung down from the horse. He went to her to hold her, to press her against the oak tree behind her and kiss her deeply, feeling the press of her breasts, of her long tapered thighs.

"You did come back."

"Possibly only to say good-bye," Ki said honestly.

"Then let us make it a fine good-bye," Nati said, turning her eyes away, letting her fingers trail down Ki's chest. "Do you remember the place down by the river?"

"Of course. I couldn't forget it."

"Nor could I. Only this time, I promise Skull will not be there. He is at the feast, eating, drinking so that he can hardly stand."

"Even Skull couldn't dissuade me," Ki said.

"No?"

"No." He kissed her curious face and together they started off toward the tiny creek, toward their hidden nook in the willows. The sky was orange and pale purple, dusk settling rapidly. The night breeze was warm now that the storm had drifted away.

In the thicket Nati undressed, very slowly, very tantalizingly, running her hands over her breasts and hips, letting Ki take in her lush beauty, letting his anticipation stoke the smoldering fires in his loins.

When she was through she lay down, still wearing her silver jewelry and she beckoned Ki to her.

He kicked off his shoes and tugged at his shirt. Then he sank to his knees and went to Nati, kissing her softly pulsing belly, her breasts.

Laslo burst from the willow, swinging the club with skull-crushing violence. Ki ducked but still the pole in Laslo's hands rang off Ki's head. He could hear Nati's scream echoing distantly like a shout in a long iron pipe. As Ki was falling, he saw Laslo strike her with the side of his fist, saw Nati drop to the earth.

Laslo was hovering over Ki. "You thought I was dead, didn't you? Thought you had finished Laslo!" Laslo's voice was not normal. His face was blistered and scabbed; his shirt was torn open at the shoulders. He was blackened and filthy and his eyes stared out wildly from a contorted, whiskered face.

"You thought I was dead, but I showed you, didn't I? I survived that fall from the bluff and then I crawled away through the ashes, through the cactus and over rocks, and then I began walking, moving only at night. I knew I would find you again no matter how long it took. And now I have!"

He swung his club again and Ki, his head still ringing,

just managed to roll to one side, the club striking his thigh painfully.

"How can I go home now? What can I do?" Laslo shouted. "They won't take me back now that I've failed!"

With an inhuman scream Laslo came in again. Ki rolled to his feet and kicked out with savage intensity. His heel struck Laslo below the heart and the cartel officer stopped in his tracks, his eyes bulging from his lumpy head. He lifted a finger as if to admonish Ki, as if to point to a distant, dark ideal, a reason for it all . . . and then he just dropped to the earth dead, his heart stilled.

Ki stood over Laslo for a long while, looking down into that hate-twisted boyish face. Then he dragged him nearer to the river where he left him with a *shuriken* resting on his chest, marking him for what he was.

Then Ki turned and went back to the thicket to say his long good-bye to Nati who waited there.

Watch for

LONE STAR AND THE GOLD MINE WAR

thirty-eighth novel in the exciting
LONE STAR
series from Jove

coming in October!

☆ From the Creators of LONGARM ☆

The Wild West will never be the same!

LONE★STAR

LONE STAR features the extraordinary and beautiful Jessica Starbuck and her loyal half-American half-Japanese martial arts sidekick, Ki.

__ LONE STAR ON THE TREACHERY TRAIL #1	07519-1/$2.50
__ LONE STAR AND THE OPIUM RUSTLERS #2	07520-5/$2.50
__ LONE STAR AND THE KANSAS WOLVES #4	07419-5/$2.50
__ LONE STAR AND THE UTAH KID #5	07415-2/$2.50
__ LONE STAR AND THE LAND GRABBERS #6	07426-8/$2.50
__ LONE STAR IN THE TALL TIMBER #7	07542-6/$2.50
__ LONE STAR AND THE HARDROCK PAYOFF #9	07643-0/$2.50
__ LONE STAR AND THE RENEGADE COMANCHES #10	07541-8/$2.50
__ LONE STAR ON OUTLAW MOUNTAIN #11	08198-1/$2.50
__ LONE STAR AND THE GOLD RAIDERS #12	08162-0/$2.50
__ LONE STAR AND THE DENVER MADAM #13	08219-8/$2.50
__ LONE STAR AND THE RAILROAD WAR #14	07888-3/$2.50
__ LONE STAR AND THE MEXICAN STANDOFF #15	07887-5/$2.50
__ LONE STAR AND THE BADLANDS WAR #16	08199-X/$2.50
__ LONE STAR AND THE SAN ANTONIO RAID #17	07353-9/$2.50
__ LONE STAR AND THE GHOST PIRATES #18	08095-0/$2.50
__ LONE STAR ON THE OWLHOOT TRAIL #19	07409-8/$2.50
__ LONE STAR ON THE DEVIL'S TRAIL #20	07436-5/$2.50
__ LONE STAR AND THE APACHE REVENGE #21	07533-7/$2.50
__ LONE STAR AND THE TEXAS GAMBLER #22	07628-7/$2.50
__ LONE STAR AND THE HANGROPE HERITAGE #23	07734-8/$2.50
__ LONE STAR AND THE MONTANA TROUBLES #24	07748-8/$2.50
__ LONE STAR AND THE MOUNTAIN MAN #25	07880-8/$2.50

Prices may be slightly higher in Canada.

Available at your local bookstore or return this form to:

JOVE
Book Mailing Service
P.O. Box 690, Rockville Centre, NY 11571

Please send me the titles checked above. I enclose _____ Include 75¢ for postage and handling if one book is ordered; 25¢ per book for two or more not to exceed $1.75. California, Illinois, New York and Tennessee residents please add sales tax.

NAME_____

ADDRESS_____

CITY_____ STATE/ZIP_____

(allow six weeks for delivery)   54

☆ **From the Creators of LONGARM** ☆

The Wild West will never be the same!

LONE STAR features the extraordinary and beautiful Jessica Starbuck and her loyal half-American, half-Japanese martial arts sidekick, Ki.

_ LONE STAR AND   07920-0/$2.50
THE STOCKYARD SHOWDOWN #26
_ LONE STAR AND   07916-2/$2.50
THE RIVERBOAT GAMBLERS #27
_ LONE STAR AND   08055-1/$2.50
THE MESCALERO OUTLAWS #28
_ LONE STAR AND THE AMARILLO RIFLES #29   08082-9/$2.50
_ LONE STAR AND   08110-8/$2.50
THE SCHOOL FOR OUTLAWS #30
_ LONE STAR ON THE TREASURE RIVER #31   08043-8/$2.50
_ LONE STAR AND THE MOON TRAIL FEUD #32   08174-4/$2.50
_ LONE STAR AND THE GOLDEN MESA #33   08191-4/$2.50
_ LONE STAR AND THE RIO GRANDE BANDITS #34   08255-4/$2.50
_ LONE STAR AND THE BUFFALO HUNTERS #35   08233-3/$2.50

Prices may be slightly higher in Canada.

Available at your local bookstore or return this form to:

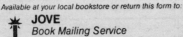 **JOVE**
Book Mailing Service
P.O. Box 690, Rockville Centre, NY 11571

Please send me the titles checked above. I enclose _____. Include 75¢ for postage and handling if one book is ordered; 25¢ per book for two or more not to exceed $1.75. California, Illinois, New York and Tennessee residents please add sales tax.

NAME_____

ADDRESS_____

CITY_____STATE/ZIP_____

(Allow six weeks for delivery.)   54

LONGARM

Explore the exciting Old West with one of the men who made it wild!

__06629-X	LONGARM ON THE HUMBOLDT #28	$2.25
__08062-4	LONGARM AND THE LAREDO LOOP #33	$2.50
__07727-5	LONGARM AND THE BLUE NORTHER #35	$2.50
__08063-2	LONGARM ON THE SANTA FE #36	$2.50
__08060-8	LONGARM AND THE STALKING CORPSE #37	$2.50
__08064-0	LONGARM AND THE COMANCHEROS #38	$2.50
__07412-8	LONGARM AND THE DEVIL'S RAILROAD #39	$2.50
__07413-6	LONGARM IN SILVER CITY #40	$2.50
__07070-X	LONGARM ON THE BARBARY COAST #41	$2.25
__07538-8	LONGARM AND THE MOONSHINERS #42	$2.50
__07431-4	LONGARM IN BOULDER CANYON #44	$2.50
__07543-4	LONGARM IN DEADWOOD #45	$2.50
__07425-X	LONGARM AND THE GREAT TRAIN ROBBERY #46	$2.50
__07418-7	LONGARM IN THE BADLANDS #47	$2.50
__07414-4	LONGARM IN THE BIG THICKET #48	$2.50
__07522-1	LONGARM AND THE EASTERN DUDES #49	$2.50
__07854-9	LONGARM IN THE BIG BEND #50	$2.50
__07523-X	LONGARM AND THE SNAKE DANCERS #51	$2.50
__07722-4	LONGARM ON THE GREAT DIVIDE #52	$2.50
__08101-9	LONGARM AND THE BUCKSKIN ROGUE #53	$2.50
__07723-2	LONGARM AND THE CALICO KID #54	$2.50
__07545-0	LONGARM AND THE FRENCH ACTRESS #55	$2.50

Prices may be slightly higher in Canada.

Available at your local bookstore or return this form to:

JOVE
Book Mailing Service
P.O. Box 690, Rockville Centre, NY 11571

Please send me the titles checked above. I enclose _____ Include 75¢ for postage and handling if one book is ordered; 25¢ per book for two or more not to exceed $1.75. California, Illinois, New York and Tennessee residents please add sales tax.

NAME_____

ADDRESS_____

CITY_____ STATE/ZIP_____
(allow six weeks for delivery.)

5

The hottest trio in Western history is riding your way in these giant

LONGARM

adventures!

The Old West Will Never be the Same Again!!!

The matchless lawman LONGARM teams up with the fabulous duo Jessie and Ki of LONE STAR fame for exciting Western tales that are not to be missed!

___08218-X LONGARM AND THE LONE STAR LEGEND	$2.95
___07085-8 LONGARM AND THE LONE STAR VENGEANCE	$2.95
___08168-X LONGARM AND THE LONE STAR BOUNTY	$2.95
___08250-3 LONGARM AND THE LONE STAR RESCUE	$3.50

Prices may be slightly higher in Canada.

Available at your local bookstore or return this form to:

 JOVE
Book Mailing Service
P.O. Box 690, Rockville Centre, NY 11571

Please send me the titles checked above. I enclose _____ Include 75¢ for postage and handling if one book is ordered; 25¢ per book for two or more not to exceed $1.75. California, Illinois, New York and Tennessee residents please add sales tax.

NAME_____

ADDRESS_____

CITY_____STATE/ZIP_____

(allow six weeks for delivery)   **45**